ABOUT THE AUTHOR

hael Humfrey was born on a banana estate in
nada. He joined the British Colonial Police Service
l served as an Assistant Superintendent in what was
t n the Uganda Protectorate. He returned to the
C ibbean four years later, became Head of the Jamaican
S rity Intelligence Branch and then Deputy
C missioner of the Jamaica Constabulary. He retired
p aturely in order to write about the West Indies. He
is authority on marine molluscs and author of *Sea
Shc of the West Indies. Portrait of a Sea Urchin* is his
acc nt of his childhood in the Caribbean. *A Gift for
An na* is his fourth novel and his short stories have
apl ed in the London Magazine and in literary
ma nes in the United States, Canada, Australia and
New Zealand.

By the same author

Novels

A Kind of Armour
A Shadow in the Weave
No Tears for Massa's Day

A Memoir

Portrait of a Sea Urchin

Short Stories

Cameron's Butterfly and other stories
In the Picture and other stories

Non-fiction

Sea Shells of the West Indies

A Gift For Angelina
a novel of the West Indies

Michael Humfrey

Matador
5 Weir Road
Kibworth Beauchamp
Leicester LE8 0LQ, UK
Tel: (+44) 116 279 2299
Fax: (+44) 116 279 2277
Email: books@troubador.co.uk
Web: www.troubador.co.uk/matador

ISBN 978 1848 764 347

Typeset in 11pt Book Antiqua by Troubador Publishing Ltd, Leicester, UK

Printed in Great Britain by the MPG Books Group, Bodmin and King's Lynn

Matador is an imprint of Troubador Publishing Ltd

For Chrissy
- with boundless love -
this story of my islands

I settled in my imagination on the perfect island. About ten years ago I went back there again by chance, while searching the Caribbean to see if any of it was left as once I knew it. A runway for jumbo jets had been built on my Eden, and the island was covered by hotels, boarding houses, boutiques, eateries, villas and hordes of tourists. Progress: absolute ruin.

Martha Gellhorn
(Afterword to *Liana*, Virago Modern Classics 1986)

CHAPTER I

It rained the afternoon that Justine left me; by six o'clock the rain had turned to snow. The flat was cold when I let myself in. I dialled up the heat but the malevolent English winter, to which I had never really adjusted, seemed to reach through the window panes to seek me out. In the street below, I could see the wavering lights of the evening traffic heading home; already there was an inch of snow on the grass behind the railings of the square. The black metal of the padlocked gate glinted under its skin of ice.

I poured myself a drink, recovered Justine's letter from the wastebasket where I had thrown it and walked into the bedroom. I stood for a moment beside the bed we had shared for more than eight years and smoothed the creases from the pale green sheet of paper with the fingers of both hands.

The top of her dressing table had been cleared. She had left only a box of paper tissues, a little filigree brooch which I had given her before we were married, and the familiar, lingering scent of her cologne. At the base of the mirror there was a fresh smear of lipstick which matched exactly the shell pink of the paper tissues. It was her favourite colour. I sat down on the unmade bed. In the brittle light that filtered through the window, I began to read the letter again:

'Darling', she had written in her firm, upright hand, 'I am leaving for Faro tonight with Luis and some friends. We want to have a look at a new complex in Albufeira. I really don't know what will happen after that, we may go on to Madeira. Luis has a house there. Be patient with me, please, as always...'

For the second time that evening I crushed the sheet of paper in my hands. I did not intend to read it again: there would be no need.

I lay down on the bed and tried to bring some order to my thoughts. As always, I could feel no bitterness towards Justine: what bitterness I felt was directed inwards. There had been other Luis's, other parties of friends and other buildings which required inspection: it had happened before. I was suddenly overwhelmed by a sense of my own failure to make her need me as I had come to need her, and by a wretchedness which I knew the brandy would be powerless to dispel.

'I think it must be a kind of wanderlust,' she had once explained after an absence of more than three weeks. 'It doesn't mean I don't love you. I could never be married to anyone else. I would always come back to you. But I have a need of other people – and sometimes life seems so short...'

I asked whether my own hurt meant nothing to her. She had turned away without answering me; but in the oval mirror on the bedroom wall, I had seen the reflection of her face bright with excitement induced by my jealousy.

'I need it all,' she said.

I lay back on the bed and closed my eyes. At first, I could think only of the touch of my wife and the ache of my own need for her. Then haltingly, imperceptibly as I lay there on the bed, my thoughts began to drift backwards down the corridor of the years to a bittersweet, familiar memory of my childhood. I was a boy again on my father's West Indian estate. It was early afternoon and the untidy ranks of ripening bananas quivered in the September heat. I turned my skewbald pony towards the stream that meandered across our land. A grove of bamboo straddled the stream, the green, segmented stems meeting in a Gothic ceiling fifty feet above the water. I tethered the pony to a fallen log and entered the cool cathedral of the bamboo. On the polished surface of the stream, a fleet of water skaters glided lightly over the reflection of my sunburnt face. I listened to the muted, hypnotic voice of the water. Wild jasmine sprang from the opposite bank and the fragrance of the white flowers had been trapped within the grove. On the gravel bed of the stream I could make out the familiar cobweb patterns traced by the crayfish which lived there. As my face loomed above them, they fled to the sanctuary of the overhanging roots. The afternoon sunlight, filtering through the roof of leaves far above me, decorated the water with little mirrors of gold.

I cupped my hands, gathered some of the cool water and splashed it across my face. The skaters fled downstream. I fetched a twig from beneath the carpet of fallen leaves and flung it into the water: it was captured by the current, spun in a tight circle and swept away between two water-worn cylinders of rock to the sea.

I could remember how I lay back on the carpet of leaves and wondered for the first time where the currents of my own life might carry me. I was old enough, I think, to sense that life had already been kind to me: I was suddenly convinced that it could only get kinder with each passing year. It was the bright certainty of that conviction which overwhelmed me with a spasm of happiness so intense that it has remained etched deep upon my memory ever since.

I propped another pillow under my head. Justine had forgotten her nightdress beneath it. I caressed the silk with the tips of my fingers. Like the room itself, it was fragrant with the scent of her body.

I thought how, all my life, I had loved beautiful things. One of my earliest memories was of gathering shells with my young nurse on the crescent beach beneath the limestone cliff on which our estate house had been built.

'Massa Carston,' the girl would protest each time without conviction, 'yuh couldn' really want to fill up yuh room wid all dem t'ings...'

4

But from the beginning I had been captivated by their form and colour, and by the prodigal way in which the sea scattered them over the sand, as if their beauty was of no significant account.

'We can wash off the sand first,' I used to plead, and Serafina would relent and help me carry them all to my bedroom in the folds of her apron.

In time, as I grew older, I assembled a vast collection of shells, displaying them upon every available surface in my room, since I could never bear to hide their beauty away unseen in cardboard boxes. I grouped them not by class and genus – even when I had learnt about such things – but in arrangements of contrasting and complementing shapes and colours. At night, after my mother had extinguished the yellow flame of the oil lamp in its bracket on the wall, I would reach up from my pillow to select one of my two precious fallow deer cowries from the shelf above my head. Then, in the darkness, I would explore the cool, polished, porcellanous surface of the exquisite shell.

One of our closest neighbours had been an old bachelor whose own estate house overlooked the sea a few miles further down the coast. Once every three months, he would invite us all to spend the afternoon with him. There would be a choice of three different kinds of tea and, precisely at five o'clock, a young black man-servant would wheel in a trolley laden with cake and delicately cut sandwiches and little yellow biscuits with pink icing which I had seen nowhere else.

The drawing room in which tea was served was

elegantly furnished. There were fine pictures on the walls and, in one corner, there was a glass-topped mahogany cabinet which displayed the owner's favourite bibelots. Once – responding to my shy request – the old man was persuaded to take a key from a chain at his waist and raise the lid.

Among the disparate objects so artfully arranged on the green baize, there was an exquisite Meissen figurine of a pink-cheeked milkmaid with pale gold hair. Of all the treasures in the cabinet, this was my own favourite. Noting my interest, the old man had reached inside, picked up the delicate piece of porcelain and placed it in my hands. Very carefully, almost reverently, I had passed the tips of my fingers over the golden hair and the finely modelled features; then I returned her safely to my host. The porcelain had been light and cool to the touch, and I never forgot the moment.

Our estate consisted of a strip of land which nowhere along its length extended more than half a mile inland from the sea. But it was not its situation which handicapped all my father's efforts to make the place profitable: it was the acid nature of the rust red soil which stunted the growth of the bananas and, at crop time, caused the American Fruit Company to reject as many bunches as they agreed to buy.

The hurricane season on Manzanilla lasted from July to September, and each year my father would say lightly: 'Can't afford to insure the crop again this season. Let's keep our fingers crossed and don't offend the weather gods.'

He would make a joke of it, but always those long, torpid months were made anxious for us by the unspoken knowledge that, in the space of half a morning, everything might be lost.

I never thought it ironic that my father should have christened our estate Sans Souci.

I never really wanted to be a journalist; in fact I had decided early on that I would be a painter. At school I had shown a certain talent and my pencil sketches were admired by my teachers. Only later did I realise that they would have had little to compare my work with and that their praise was overblown.

Not long after the end of the Second World War – which had scarcely touched our way of life in the West Indies – my mother came into a legacy from an aunt who had loved her. It was enough to send me to art college in London. I took up my place there on my twentieth birthday but, by the end of that first year, it was clear to everyone that I lacked any distinctive gift. It was agreed that I had a natural sense of colour and balance, but somehow I could never master the proper use of perspective. There were better artists on the pavement outside the National Gallery. It was the first of my disappointments – the first clear evidence that life, after all, was not bound to grow sweeter with each passing year. This realisation was made more painful, I think, by the discovery that journalism – which I had taken up almost by accident – came easily to me and seemed to be what I was meant to do for a living. By the time I was 24, I had a good job with a London evening newspaper and three rooms of my own overlooking the river.

At Sans Souci, things had gone badly after I left. In August the weather gods at last withdrew their favour and the tail-end of a hurricane flattened that year's banana crop. My mother's letters became increasingly despondent and, at the beginning of the next year, my father wrote to say that the banks were calling in their loans. The estate was sold and my parents returned unhappily to a country they scarcely recognised and to a terraced house in a Suffolk market town. Neither of them was ever able to come to terms with the loss of that narrow strip of Manzanillan land where I was born and which I loved so much in spite of its unfruitful soil. My father died two years later and my mother not long afterwards. I moved on to another newspaper and a better job.

Time passed agreeably enough for me. If I was aware that there was a certain emptiness at the centre of my life – a lack of fulfilment – I did not allow it to interfere with the way I lived. I still carried with me in my car a little sketch pad and a few pastel crayons, but I hardly ever made serious use of them because the result always served to remind me of what I could never be.

One of the aspects of my job I most enjoyed was writing a fortnightly column which appeared on an inside page. I had decided one month to prepare a piece about trends in the design of office buildings, and I had gone to seek the view of an architect friend who held strong opinions about his own profession. He met me on the steps of the building where he worked and took me inside. A girl was sitting at a large table in the centre of the room as we walked in, a wayward strand of pale gold hair falling lightly over the drawing in front of her. She was sketching what looked to me like a gently curving flight of stairs. She glanced up as I passed by and our eyes met. Hers returned to the task in front of her: mine evidently betrayed my admiration because, as we entered his office, my friend said facetiously: 'I better tell you at once – you'd be wasting your time there. That one is saving herself for Mr Right...'

I was not discouraged, guessing correctly as it turned out, that my friend had reasons of his own for deflecting another man's interest.

'All the same,' I remember saying evenly as I sat down at his desk, 'you could introduce me when I leave...' and before he could frame an evasion, Justine knocked lightly at the door and walked in with her sketch in her hand. She had not known I was still there. My friend introduced us. I offered to wait outside. She studied me closely for a moment without expression: then in that soft, clear voice which I was soon to know so well – and which could turn at unexpected moments to a deeper, more urgent tone – she said: 'Thank you, but that really isn't necessary. I can come back later.'

Before I could insist, she smiled at me, turned on her sandaled heel and closed the door behind her. A trace of her cologne hung lightly in the air after she had gone. My friend said nothing. We passed on to the subject of my visit and his views on the banality of contemporary office design. It was not a useful interview.

I had telephoned Justine when I returned to my own

office and asked her to the theatre. I think she was expecting me to call. Two weeks later we made love for the first time. My friend had lied: she had not been saving herself for anyone.

Afterwards, when I had delivered her safely back to her own flat next morning, I found myself recalling two things especially about her: the sea green colour of her eyes, and the shape of her feet. In my experience, most women have ugly feet: it was a fact that always troubled me. Over the years I had learnt never to look at their feet while I undressed them, in case it served to dull the edge of my desire.

Justine's feet, however, were exactly in keeping with the rest of her. They were delicate and finely shaped. I discovered at once that I could look at them with pleasure and excitement, in the same way that I looked at her long-nippled breasts and the flawless oval of her face.

Early one morning as I drove back to my flat – she would never stay the whole night with me – the thought occurred that it was as if that exquisite, golden-haired porcelain milkmaid I had once longed to own had somehow come to life and could now be mine forever,

Not long after that, we spent a weekend at a small hotel in the Norfolk countryside. On our way back to London that Sunday evening, I turned off the main road and drew up in the entrance to a farmer's field. We sat there in silence under the curious gaze of a herd of black and white bullocks. The summer's evening was full of the fragrance of cropped grass and the warm smell of the cattle. I asked Justine to marry me. Two hours later, as we drew up outside her flat, she leant over and kissed me hard on the mouth. 'Yes,' she said. 'Yes, I think I will.'

I knew of course when we married that Justine had a wide and cherished circle of friends and that at least half of these were men. I had imagined that these people – whatever they had once been to her – would now take their places in the background of her life. I soon saw that I was wrong.

Once, when we had been married less than six months, I returned home unexpectedly in the middle of the morning to collect a draft I had forgotten in my study. Justine had taken a day off from her job and there was a man in the sitting room. The man had a drink in his hand and his tie was undone. Without embarrassment, Justine introduced him as an old friend. Shortly afterwards, he made his excuses and left; but later that evening, while we were eating, there was a telephone call for Justine. When she returned to the table, her eyes were bright with a kind of animal excitement.

I asked her who it was and, without a moment's hesitation, she said: 'It was Bobby; you met him this morning. He's left his wife...'

There were other telephone calls from time to time when I was there and, occasionally, there was evidence that other men came to the flat when I was at work. Justine never sought to deny it.

'Oh, yes', she would say. 'I had a morning off and Simon came round. I've known him for years. You met him at the party after our wedding. He's in London for a few days...' And then she would take my hands in hers and add: 'You know they're all my friends. Don't be jealous, darling. They've been part of my life for a long time now.'

Then she would reach up and kiss me and move her body against mine until, dark with desire for her, I would gather her up in my arms and carry her to our bed. There, with her long, pale gold hair spread in careless disorder across the pillow, she would whisper: 'It's only you I really love, it 's only you...' and once again she would be my porcelain milkmaid come to life and everything I had ever wanted.

CHAPTER II

I woke cold and stiff next morning in the armchair where I had spent the night. My first conscious thought was that I must get away from London for a while. I did not want to stay alone in the empty flat as I had done in the past, and I couldn't face the awkward sympathy of colleagues who would soon learn that Justine had left me once again.

It was in this state of mind when the thought first occurred to me that I might find comfort of some sort in the one place where my life had never been touched by unhappiness – the island on which I had been born. I would take what leave was due to me and I would stay on Manzanilla until Justine tired of Luis and came home.

I telephoned my editor to claim the five weeks leave I was owed. I suggested the name of a colleague who could be asked to take over my work at short notice.

The editor made no attempt to conceal his displeasure.

'You should have given me more notice,' he complained. 'It's inconvenient at the moment and you know it. And your column's due at the end of the week...'

'It's a family matter,' I said. 'I can't put it off...'

'Well, five weeks,' he said ungraciously. 'And please, not a day more – and send me a note saying where we can reach you if we have to.'

I booked a flight to Manzanilla and a hotel room in the capital. I began to pack a suitcase. I laid carefully among my shirts, so that its silver frame should not be damaged, the photograph of Justine which I had kept on my study desk since the day we returned from our honeymoon. It had been her wedding present to me, and she had inscribed it with her everlasting love. Out of habit, I threw in at the same time my sketch pad and a sheaf of pastel crayons. In the street outside, it had begun to snow again.

The aircraft left from Gatwick later that evening and I slept fitfully in my seat.

I had been away from Manzanilla for more than twenty years. The island was independent now and, from time to time, I would see in the Sunday magazines advertisements for Manzanillan hotels which had been built in places where there were only empty beaches when I was a boy. A colleague in my office had stayed at one of these hotels. He had not enjoyed his holiday and I asked him why. 'They don't seem to like us there,' he said, and I had left it at that.

From the air, my first impression was that nothing had changed. Far below, I could make out the little archipelago of coral cays which hung like a necklace from the hooked peninsular at the eastern end of Manzanilla. The channels between the cays were a shifting, luminous shade of green – the exact colour, I thought, of Justine's eyes in the half light of morning. Then the cays were left behind us and the aircraft turned to follow the gentle curve of the Manzanillan coastline. Through the window opposite my seat, I could see the familiar, wooded range of mountains which ran down the centre of the island. A thin mist drifted over the summit of the range and the valleys were shrouded in a soft blue haze. We passed low over the harbour of the capital and prepared to land.

The immigration officer admitted me for thirty days to the place where I was born. I saw the point of his pencil hover for a moment above this piece of information in my passport; he looked briskly at the photograph and then at my face. Without a word, he pushed the passport back towards me across the pitted wooden counter. I collected my case from the customs bench and walked through the doors at the far end of the hall. As I stepped out of the shadow of the building, a wave of reflected heat seemed to rise up from the concrete pavement and enfold me in its grasp. The file of decrepit taxis parked against the kerb shimmered and twisted in the broad sea of light. I sat down for a moment in the shade of a pollarded almond tree and fumbled in my case for my sunglasses. A gust of wind, like the breath of an open furnace, drove an empty plastic bag across the concrete towards me. The bag came to rest at the base of the tree and wrapped itself about a ragged accumulation of discarded rubbish.

Beyond the line of taxis, a coach drew up to disgorge a small group of white tourists on their way home. They all wore identical shirts with palm tree motifs, and straw hats which bore the name of their hotel in purple letters. Their speech was laced with a spurious idiom which they had picked up from the beach boys and enjoyed using among themselves.

A man with rimless spectacles beat out a faltering rhythm on a drum which he had slung around his neck. The group formed a ragged conga line as they moved off towards the departure lounge for one last rum punch. The black coach driver, who had brought the party from their hotel, lit a marijuana cigarette and leant back against the side of his vehicle to watch them go. As the last cavorting figure disappeared inside the building, I saw him count the money he had collected from the passengers; then he spat quietly in the gutter.

I hailed one of the taxis and gave the driver the name of my hotel in the capital. We drove out along the narrow strip of land that formed one arm of the harbour basin. It was a place we used to visit when I was a boy to watch the ships pass in the deep water channel three hundred yards from shore. We picnicked there and cast for jack crevalle from the beach. I saw now that the beach had become a graveyard for discarded vehicles: their decaying bodies advanced some distance into the green water, their bonnets sprung open and eaten away by rust. Among them, the headless corpse of a dog lay stranded by the tide, the exposed rib cage very white against the oil-stained sand.

We left the long spit of land and turned west to join

the coastal road. The road ran beside a cement factory; a crooked plume of dense white smoke issued from its chimney. The wheels of the taxi raised a tail of dust behind us. There had been a screen of mangroves just here at the water's edge, but there was no trace now of that living green wall and the harbour water, with its bright sheen of oil and curdled flotsam, lapped right up against the ragged margin of the road.

We entered the outskirts of the capital. I remembered neat clapboard bungalows on either side of the road, with bougainvillea and alamanda in the front gardens and star apple trees overhanging the pavement. Now, there was only neglect. Pyramids of rubbish festered in the afternoon sun. Many of the bungalows were derelict and groups of sullen men were gathered outside a succession of rum bars. The air was full of the insistent beat of rap music and the stench of marijuana. The taxi drew up at a traffic signal. A boy of fifteen or sixteen put his head through the open window of the vehicle and stared at me with hostile, bloodshot eyes. 'Yuh want ganga, white man?' he inquired.

I shook my head.

'Den go back where yuh come from,' he said contemptuously. 'We nuh need yuh here...'

The elderly taxi driver did not look round.

'Yuh better turn up de window, baas,' he said laconically.

The light turned green and we moved on.

I had heard more than once in recent years that it had become unwise for visitors to walk the streets of the capital even in daylight. I had tended to discount it.

I did not do so now. From where I sat in the uncertain refuge of the taxi, the menace on those once familiar streets was unmistakable.

Ahead of us, I could see another traffic signal. I reached over and turned up my window.

My hotel lay on the northern outskirts of the city, where the broad coastal plain sloped up towards the distant mountain range. When I was a boy, the land all around had been open pasture and a giant saman tree grew where the hotel now stood. A friend of my parents had owned a weekend cottage at the edge of the savannah. The man had been a noted entomologist and had written a book describing all one hundred and thirty eight species of Manzanillan butterfly. Two or three times a year, we used to drive over the mountains to stay with him. I could remember one early morning following him through the dew-soaked paraa grass in pursuit of a rare black swallowtail which had strayed from its rightful home on the steep slopes of the mountains behind us. The entomologist had gently removed the insect from the folds of his net, measured the length of its delicate body and then released it on a gust of wind. I had never seen that particular kind of butterfly before; there had been bold arcs of red and purple on the insect's coal black wings and I remember wishing that it might have been possible to preserve that transient beauty for ever within a block of glass.

Now, as I looked from the seat of my taxi across the open space where the butterfly had been captured and released, I saw that the squat concrete hotel building was surrounded by a chain link fence capped with a roll of barbed wire. In an effort to soften its impact, the fence and its crown of wire had been painted green, but a dull patina of rust had already set in to mottle the effect.

I leant forward in my seat. 'Why the fence?' I said to the driver.

The man hesitated for a moment, then he lifted his hands off the steering wheel and made a gesture intended to encompass the whole island.

'Dis place gone to ruination,' he said softly. 'Every hotel have to fence-off now...'

I did not want to hear it. I said briskly: 'You better know that I was born here on the island...'

The driver was unimpressed. He shrugged his shoulders. 'Well, backra,' he said wearily, 'I can tell yuh don' live here now. Yuh goin' see: de whole place mash up.'

We passed through a gate in the fence attended by a security guard with a firearm at his belt. I paid the driver, booked into the hotel and followed a bell boy to my room. The boy accepted his tip without gratitude: it was clear he thought he could extract more from me and he stood his ground in the middle of the room until I walked onto the veranda that overhung the car park. I heard him say something under his breath and then close the door loudly behind him.

The hotel was almost empty. I ate dinner by myself at a table in one corner of the dining room. A middle-aged American at the table nearest me was drunk: he kept waving his glass in the air to attract the attention of his waiter. After a while the man noticed me, left his table and walked over. He put his hand on the back of my chair to steady himself. His eyes were bloodshot and I saw there was a deep purple weal running from his right eyebrow upwards to the hairline. The man put a finger carefully on the injury.

'See this?' he said thickly. 'I got mugged today – fifty feet from the hotel gate. First time it ever happened to me – and I travel all over...' He stroked the side of his face. 'You ever know such a shit of a place?' he asked.

He abandoned his table and wandered off towards the bar before I could frame a reply.

I made my way up to my room as soon as I had finished my meal. For much of the night I lay sleepless on my bed, my mind full of troubled, unwelcome images. I had not drawn the curtains and, at some point, the darkness outside was split by lightning. The rain hammered against the windows and I could hear someone moving restlessly in the room immediately above me.

When I woke next morning the rain had gone. To the north, the vertebrae of the Blue Mountains were curiously magnified by the rain-washed air. The familiar mass of the mountains seemed to rise up and tower over the sprawling city: I felt once more that I could reach out and touch their green flanks from where I stood. In the valleys, which branched like leaf veins among the lower slopes, a fine mist clung to the course of each ravine.

I ate breakfast in my room; then I went down to hire

a car. I drove out of the capital along the familiar road that still ran between untidy fields of sugar cane. The road ran north, over the spine of the Blue Mountains. I turned east, along the coast. A red and yellow bus, ferrying a handful of tourists from one hotel to another, passed by with its klaxon braying.

I remembered the road well. For several miles it ran beside an unbroken stretch of coral sand. All along the high water mark, the last full tide had cast up a tangle of lattice-work sea fans and the single valves of coon oyster shells. The shells lay heaped upon the sand like fragments of pleated white linen drying in the sun.

The road was uneven and cratered with holes. One sharp-edged fissure in the tarmac surface reached from the sandy verge almost to the crown of the road. I saw it too late. I swerved sharply and stepped hard on the brake. There was a loud report and the steering wheel pulled heavily to the left. I brought the car inelegantly to a halt at the edge of the road and got out to inspect the damage. I saw at once that the worn left front tyre was split from the rim to the margin of the tread.

I opened the boot and extracted the spare wheel and the jack. In the heat of the morning sun, I paused for a moment to gather my energy for the task of changing the wheel. On the opposite side of the road, set back a little into the undergrowth, there was an ancient guango tree. In its shadow, sprawled between the blade-like roots, I could see two men watching me as I worked. They were sharing a pipe of smouldering marijuana and they waited patiently until I had tightened the nuts on the spare wheel and was about to place the shredded tyre in the boot. Then they got to their feet, emerged from the shadow of the tree and crossed the road towards me.

'Yuh want ganga, man?' one of the men inquired briskly. He held up a stained brown paper bag.

I looked round and saw that the other man was standing against the door of the car. He was carrying a machete in his hand and he did not move as another busload of tourists went by. The car rocked gently in the slipstream of the bus.

'I don't use ganga,' I said.

'Well, yuh goin' pay us hundred dollar wedder yuh tek de weed or not,' the first man said, 'an' yuh should be glad we not chargin' more.'

There was a long moment of silence, punctuated only by the play of the waves on the beach beside the road. I looked down at the jack handle lying at my feet. The man with the machete followed my gaze and kicked the steel rod contemptuously beneath the car.

'Hundred dollar right now,' he said. He ran his fingers along the back of the machete's blade. Another vehicle passed by in a thin cloud of dust. The driver blew his horn and the man with the machete raised his hand in greeting.

'Hundred dollar,' he said again and took a step closer to me. He stank of sweat and of the drug he had been smoking.

I counted out a hundred dollars from the money I had changed at the hotel. The man took the notes from my hand and dropped the paper bag of marijuana at my feet.

'Yuh lucky is us yuh dealing wid,' he said. 'We could a tek it all – but we is not greedy...'

The men strolled casually back across the road to the shelter of the guango tree. I saw one of them recover the ganga pipe from the place where he had left it: then they seemed to disappear within the shifting patterns of light and shade beneath the heavy branches of the tree. I retrieved the jack handle from beneath the car and returned it to the boot.

I looked out to sea: some fifty yards beyond the beach there was a crescent reef, the purple blades of the gorgonians just breaking the surface of the water as the tide ran out. It was one of the reefs along the coast which I used to fish with my spear gun. I remembered one calm morning when I had speared an incautious parrot fish feeding near the surface on a blade of elkhorn coral. The barb of my spear had failed to fix itself firmly in the soft flesh and the fish had worked its way free and then taken refuge in a cavity at the base of the reef.

I had re-loaded the spear gun, filled my lungs with air and pursued the wounded fish down through the green water. I approached the entrance to the cavity and thrust the point of my spear vigorously into the blackness beyond. The fish did not come out; instead, there had been a violent eruption of sand and coral debris and the spear gun was almost torn from my grasp. Three feet in front of my face mask, its fierce eyes on fire with threat and malice, there was the bullet head of a moray eel. The coiled body, green with mucus, was thicker than my own thigh. The creature's jaws opened and closed rhythmically with an air of infinite menace.

I had made do that day with two trifling, hapless cowfish which had strayed too far from the shelter of the coral. Hannah, our old cook at Sans Souci who had known me since the day I was born, laughed openly at the sight of the puny cowfish.

'Massa Carston,' she had said, her breasts quivering with delight at her own witticism, 'yuh really should have leave a little somet'ing for dem udder fishermen to catch...'

Even so, she had baked the fish for me in red hot ash, and I had eaten them that evening with plantain and sweet potato and never told my parents about my conflict with the eel.

I got into the car and drove on. In the mirror, I could see one of the men cross the road to retrieve the paper bag from where I had left it on the ground.

The car cleaved a path through a cloud of saffron butterflies. The windscreen was stained yellow by their wing scales and by the cream extrusion from their broken bodies. I turned a switch on the dashboard and wiped the glass clean. One of the living insects was swept inside the car and settled on my shirt sleeve. I removed it delicately and held it out of the window in order to release it. The force of the slipstream tore the frail body from the wings before I had time to open my fingers. When I looked down at my hand, the fingers were stained yellow like the windscreen of the car.

The road swung abruptly to the right and passed over a familiar bridge with rusting lattice-work iron railings above the white water below. The western boundary of what had been our land lay to the left of the main road a little further on. On the far bank of the tumbling river, there had been a palm-lined drive which led up to the estate of our nearest neighbours, whose inherited wealth allowed them to be indifferent to anything the hurricane season might bring them. Their house had been built to a plan of their own design, with a double sweep of marble steps leading to a veranda with white leather arm chairs and tables piled high with copies of *Life* and the *New Yorker* and the *National Geographic* magazine. The garden was studded with beds of bougainvillea and coral hibiscus, and there were pale pink lilies floating in the guppy ponds set in the green expanse of lawn. They spent the hot months of the year at their other house on Martha's Vineyard and, though we waved to each other when we passed on the main road, they were always chauffeur driven. They belonged to a different world, and we knew it.

In the hired car, I was suddenly aware that the steering wheel was slippery in my grasp. The palms of my hands were wet with sweat and, above the clatter of the engine, I thought I could hear the beat of my heart. I breathed deeply in a futile attempt to calm myself; then I turned sharp left off the main road towards the sea and the place where I was born.

It had never occurred to me that here, too, all might be changed. Inevitably, I knew, another owner would have altered certain features of the estate: bananas might well have given place to a more profitable crop; some of the work might now be done with tractors. But somehow I had taken it for granted that the house itself and the contours of the land would still look much the same as they had done when I lived there. I had never thought that I might be unable to recognise any of it.

It took several minutes before I was able to convince myself that I had not taken the wrong turning from the main road. I looked about me for familiar landmarks. On the grass-cloaked rise where our house had stood there was now only the squat bulk of a hotel. The hotel had grey concrete walls and there were narrow, half-glazed balconies projecting from each room over the grey concrete apron beneath them. On the flat roof of the structure above the entrance there was a giant, winking neon sign, and it was this that told me at once that I had made no mistake: WELCOME TO THE PLACE WITHOUT CARE, it read. Beyond the electric sign an arc of flags had been planted. In the morning sunlight the flags and the pulsating gentian letters of the sign made a show of colour against the slab walls of the building, but they could do nothing to reduce its intrusive ugliness.

Like the hotel in the capital where I had spent the night, this one too was defended by a chain link fence and rusting coils of barbed wire. The land in front of the hotel, which I remembered as an uneven field of gros michel bananas, was levelled now. It had been born again as a putting course, flat and featureless as a baize table. The stream, which once meandered without purpose across the estate to the sea, had been taken in hand: it bisected the putting course now in a dead straight line, dammed at intervals to serve as a series of water hazards. Two middle-aged men and a woman in lycra shorts were playing on the course as I looked. Of the grove of whispering bamboo which had sheltered me and my dreams beside the water, there was no trace at all. The general area lay buried beneath the tarmac apron of the hotel's car park, but it was impossible in that transfigured landscape to be certain just where the bamboo might have grown.

I parked the car and walked towards the hotel. A concrete footpath led round the side of the building to the beach. The footpath gave way to a spiral of narrow steps cut into the face of the cliff. At the bottom, I stepped onto the sand. I saw at once that, above the high water mark, the random groves of manchineel and broad-leafed sea grape had been rooted out. In their place, at precisely measured intervals, there was now a succession of identical concrete platforms. Each platform was shaded by a purple beach umbrella and furnished with a circle of yellow plastic chairs. Beyond the concrete platforms there was a tall metal mast with a clutch of loudspeakers fixed to its apex. The hard beat of reggae music echoed over the water. The concrete platforms were beginning to fill up with people. The smell of sun tan oil hung on the air.

I began to walk down the length of the beach. It was apparent at once that the sand from one end of the crescent to the other had been raked clean earlier that morning. At the far end of the beach I could see a tractor at rest beneath its own plastic umbrella. The machine had done a thorough job: as a result of its labours there were no shells to be seen on that beach, no water-worn fragments of coral, not even a stranded frond of sargasso weed to mark the limit of the night's high tide. The beach, whose cast up treasures had brought me such delight when I was a boy, was as barren now as the face of the moon. Overwhelmed by a sense of irretrievable loss, I found myself hurrying back up the steps in the face of the cliff to the place where I had left the car.

On the narrow path I brushed past a Rastafarian carrying a plastic bag of marijuana cigarettes for sale on the beach. The man turned to protest but I scarcely heard him. In the car park, the black surface of the tarmac was melting under the mid-day sun. I took one final look at the place where I was born: only the words of the neon sign suggested that we had ever lived there. We had left no other mark.

I drove into the mountains. The road I followed was narrow and uneven; it clung tightly to the contours of the foothills, so that each hairpin bend was succeeded by another sharper and steeper still. It threw its coils around the precipitous sides of the mountains like some constricting serpent. The air grew cooler. The groves of white cedar gave place to larger, more exotic trees. From time to time, a decrepit country bus approached from the opposite direction, holding fiercely to the crown of the road, forcing me to a halt on the rough grass verge beyond which there was nothing but the sheer side of the mountain.

When I had put a sufficient distance between myself and the squat hotel which had obliterated Sans Souci, I pulled into a clearing at the side of the road. The clearing lay in the shadow of a julie mango tree. I switched off the engine, climbed out of the car and breathed deeply. The fragrance of fallen mangoes hung in the air, the sweet, cloying scent of the over-ripe fruit released on the damp earth by the wheels of the car. There had been a julie mango tree just beyond the windows of my bedroom at Sans Souci. It had been possible to use it as a ladder to reach the ground from my room and it had served, too – within the cover of its branches – as a place of refuge when I wished to be alone but did not choose to visit the bamboo grove. The old tree would have been one of the first objects to feel the thrust of the bulldozer's blade when they levelled the house to make way for the new hotel and the black-topped car park beside it. The loss of the tree, I thought, was one thing: in time, I could have accepted even the destruction of the clapboard house itself. It was that sterile, shell-less beach which somehow proved too much to bear.

A minibus with a gaping headlight socket passed by on its journey to the capital. A passenger stuck her head through the unglazed window at the back and yelled at me. Above the clamour of the vehicle's engine, I caught the words: '... go back where yuh ... come from'

Like the young man in the capital who thrust his head inside my taxi, the woman wanted me to know that, outside the steel fences of the hotels, I was not welcome in Manzanilla; and that knowledge in itself made futile the whole purpose of my return to the place where I was born. There was no comfort to be found here, no catharsis and no point now in staying on. The Manzanilla of my memory had ceased to exist: what had supplanted it seemed to me both alien and unlovely.

I thought wearily of the long journey back to England and of my return to the flat, fragrant still with Justine's cologne and the echo of her presence. I would wait there now, as I had done before, until she tired of Luis and of travel and returned to me again. She would be remorseful and eager. In a curious way, my hurt always excited her sexually and I would take her back on her own terms, as she knew I would, because she was everything to me and I could not live without her. Then, inexorably, after a month or so her attention would turn once more from me to other pleasures and, in time, to other men, and the cycle would repeat itself and nothing would have changed.

A familiar blanket of longing and despair settled over me there in the car, beneath the laden branches of the mango tree. I looked without hope across the green foothills of the mountain range to the sea and onwards to the arc of the distant horizon and beyond.

Then I remembered Angelina.

CHAPTER III

On a detailed map of the Caribbean, Angelina can be seen as a fleck of green in the blue expanse of sea due north of Haiti. It is strung like a jewel on the thread of the twenty first parallel.

Because of its position on the old sea route to Hispaniola, the island had appeared on the earliest charts of the conquistadores. The Spanish navigators pricked it down as Angel de la Guarda: by the middle of the seventeenth century when, with Manzanilla itself, it was taken by Penn and Venables for the Commonwealth, the island had already become known simply as Angelina and it soon took its place under this name on subsequent maps of the West Indies. For three hundred years it remained under the jurisdiction of the British Governor of Manzanilla, but in all those years only two of them had ever considered the place worth visiting and there had never been any European settlement.

I owed what little I knew about Angelina to my father's love of fishing. He had never been able to afford a boat of his own, but some of his friends owned fishing vessels and, from time to time, they would invite him to go with them when they put to sea. As a special treat to mark my sixteenth birthday, my father arranged for me to crew on a neighbour's boat to fish the deep water north of Cap Haitien. There, in the dead season of the planter's year, we trolled for tuna and dog-toothed ocean gar.

On the second day, our course took us within sight of Angelina. As I had never landed there, it was planned that we would all go ashore on the little island late in the afternoon. That morning, however, the tuna moved off to the west and, without debate, we followed the fish into the Windward Passage. Angelina was lost in the midday haze astern of us. When we returned to Manzanilla two days later, I was left only with a tantalising memory of the little island's saddle-backed silhouette and the tall limestone cliffs which rose sheer from the sea to a green mantle of rain forest.

'What's it like on the island?' I had asked as the tuna pressed on westwards.

My father was at the tiller and the boat's owner had just hauled in the trolling line and was baiting the hook with squid. The man put the hook down on the deck and turned to look back along our broken wake.

'Well, son,' he said thoughtfully, 'the people there are not like you and me. They're simple souls and they don't want much to do with the rest of the world. They have their own kind of life and they live it. None of them ever wants to go anywhere else. That's their choice and I guess they're entitled to it.' He picked up the hook again and tested the swivel. 'They're born, they have children and they die – and that's about all I can say of them.'

My father had been listening to us. 'They're all in-bred,' he said. 'You wouldn't know it to look at them, but maybe it explains why they keep to themselves.'

I didn't understand. 'What's in-bred?' I asked a few minutes later.

My father looked up at the set of the mainsail and explained it to me.

'Is it bad?' I wanted to know.

'I don't think it has to be,' he said. 'It used to happen in every isolated little village all over England for hundreds of years and we're not all raving yet...'

The wind swung round into the east and I went forward to loosen the jib. Before we had gone about to follow the tuna westwards, the same wind had carried out to the boat for the first time the warm, fragrant smell of the little island. When Angelina slipped beneath the rim of the horizon not long afterwards, I remember that I had felt a sharp, unaccountable sense of lost opportunity.

Now, thirty years later, as I sat disconsolate overlooking the place where I was born, it occurred to me that I was being given a second chance to visit the island – and that my brief return to the Caribbean might serve some purpose after all.

In the event, I discovered that it was going to be more difficult to reach Angelina than I might have guessed. No airstrip had been built on the island, and there was no regular service by sea. Schooners from Manzanilla called there only when there was a cargo to deliver or collect. Several weeks might pass before anyone considered the journey worthwhile. I learnt, too, that there were no hotels on Angelina, not even a simple guest house, and it was only by chance I discovered that the headman – the cacique of the island as he was called by his own people – owned a thatched bungalow which he made available to the occasional visitor who wished to see the island. There was no way of getting a message to the cacique ahead of my own arrival and, when I eventually reached the island, I knew that I might find the bungalow already let to someone else.

It took me all the following day to discover that a single masted schooner out of Port Cabrera was due to collect a cargo of copra and smoked fish from Angelina sometime the next week. I drove to the town, sought out the captain and booked my passage. Then I returned to my hotel in the capital, collected my suitcase and took a room in a guest house at Port Cabrera to wait for the schooner to sail.

I passed the next three days travelling aimlessly about Manzanilla, still hoping, I think, that I would find I had been mistaken and much was still the same. It was a despondent journey. Even in the countryside – in the villages high in the mountains – I discovered that a new generation had acquired a hard, covetous quality. It made them discontented with their own lives and envious of people who had more. It seemed to me that no one smiled now and everywhere, never far beneath the surface, I could sense that unnerving threat of violence which was the real cause of the steel fences which shut away the tourists in the antiseptic fortresses of their beach hotels.

At a place where I stopped to eat, the bar was deserted and the old barman sat idly on his stool as I walked in. I bought each of us a drink and, after a while, I asked him about the other white families who had owned estates on Manzanilla when I was a boy. It seemed that most of them had sold up and left not long after independence. He thought that some had gone to New Zealand and Australia; the others just drifted away.

'Dey jus' pack up and leave,' the old man said quietly. 'Ever'ting start to change some years ago. Dey put up hotels all along de coast an' soon de islan' full of tourists. After dat, de young people jus' seem to lose dem sense of direction an' de drugs come in. De whole place different now...'

The owner of the guest house at Port Cabrera was an elderly woman with pale brown skin and tired eyes. We were sitting together on the veranda of the building after the evening meal, and I told her what I had learnt from the bartender earlier that day. Was it true? I asked.

The woman considered carefully for a moment.

'Yes,' she said. 'After independence the white planters sold up for what they could get and cleared out. The politicians borrowed money and built the big hotels. Then the people saw all the tourists coming with their cameras and their money and they looked at themselves and found that they had nothing. After that, the drugs started to arrive and then everything changed...'

She passed a hand wearily across her face. I knew that in the old days she would have belonged to the prosperous middle classes: her little, fading hotel would have been her family's house.

'People said it would be good for Manzanilla,' she said. 'Truth is we were not ready for it and this tourism business has spoiled us. We have become a bitter people and no one is satisfied any more with what life gives him. People don't trust each other: we don't like the tourists and, God help us, we don't like each other any better.'

We sat in silence for a while, watching the moon rise over the sea. 'Sometimes I wake in the night and wonder whether it is a kind of sickness we have caught,' she said. 'I am glad my husband never lived to see it...'

After a while I excused myself and made my way up the old wooden stairs to my room.

Next day I gave up my car. I had no wish to see any more of the island. The on-shore breeze failed that afternoon and a blanket of dust and heat settled low over the town. I lay naked on my bed, listening to the harsh, monotonous beat of reggae music from the bars at the water's edge.

My thoughts were all of Justine – of the colour of her hair and the curve of her belly, and of the soft animal cry she sometimes gave when I entered her. Did she do the same with Luis, I remember thinking – and with all the others whom I did not know?

In the evening, I walked down the hill from the guest house to the beach beside the decaying dock. I remembered it well. Sans Souci had not been far away.

Two or three times a month, we used to drive to that same beach in our rust-pitted, high-slung Buick to buy crab and lobster from the fishwives gathered among the canoes. I used to pass among the canoes and talk with the men as they spread out their seine nets to dry on the sand. Some of them knew that I collected shells, and they would keep for me whatever had been caught up in the folds of the net as it was hauled ashore.

'Yuh man,' someone called out now as I reached the place where the boats had once been beached. I turned to look at the boy. 'Yuh don' belong here,' he said, 'Go back to yuh hotel room'

Reluctantly, obediently, with an acute sense of final loss, I retraced my steps up the hill to the airless security of my room.

The schooner left next morning. I paid my bill, told my landlady where I was going and boarded the little vessel which lay alongside the wooden dock. An unsecured plank of white cedar served as a gangway. The crew cast off, raising the jib and mainsail together. At once the tar-stained canvas filled with the off-shore breeze. The vessel gathered way, hauling behind her the ephemeral tail of her wake. We passed out of the sheltered waters of the harbour; a burst of salt spray flew across the fo'c'sle and slapped me lightly on the cheek.

For ten dollars on top of the standard fare, the captain had lent me the use of his own cramped cabin. For much of that first morning and afternoon, I lay on his slatted wooden bunk. It was plain to me now that it had been a mistake to return to the Caribbean: I wondered how I could ever have thought any comfort could be gained by running away. I slept fitfully in the afternoon, at ease with the movement of the old vessel, but my sleep was punctuated by crude images of Justine and Luis together in Faro – or by now, perhaps, in the mountains of Madeira.

At sunset, one of the crew emerged from the galley with a bowl of curry and rice. He set the meal down on a hinged table which he drew out of the bulkhead. The goat's carcase had been carved into cubes of pink flesh. The meat was tough and pungent: I found that the half-remembered taste of goat was sharpened, not eclipsed, by the bird peppers and ginger root with which it had simmered all day over the galley fire. Afterwards, I left the cabin with its blended stench of ancient meals and unwashed clothes, to walk about the deck in the failing light.

The night was fine: a three quarter moon rose early. The sails of the schooner were filled with the moonlight and with the prevailing wind. There was a long, even swell from the east and, from time to time, the vessel drove her blunt stem deep into the sea. On either side of the bow, a school of bottlenose dolphins cut furrows of green fire into the surface of the water. Except for the helmsman, the crew had found their favoured places on the deck and were already asleep. The captain, I saw, had reserved for himself the flat roof of the galley, above the charcoal fire which still glowed softly in its grate.

I discovered a length of tarpaulin in the darkness and laid it over the rough planks of the deck. From where I lay, I could see the impassive black face of the helmsman lit by the glow of the hurricane lantern which swung in lazy circles from a hook on the backstay. The following wind had died away and the man leant backwards on a wicker chair and thrust his bare feet casually between the spokes of the wheel. Above the masthead, the night sky was pierced with stars. The schooner carried no compass and, from time to time, the helmsman glanced up at the stars to check his course.

The vessel rolled and pitched to the rhythm of the even swell. The sharp odour of countless cargoes of copra and dried fish, impregnated forever in the bruised planks beneath my head, was overlaid now by the clean smell of the open sea. I listened to the passage of the water along the side of the vessel and to the complaining song of the wood and canvas all about me. I decided to sleep where I lay on the deck.

I called to the helmsman: 'Wake me when you sight Angelina.'

The man removed a wooden toothpick from between his lips.

'O.K.,' he grunted without looking round, 'I will rouse yuh...'

I turned over on the unyielding deck, but I did not sleep. I thought again of Justine in Faro with Luis, and the pain collected in a knot beneath my heart.

I was woken at first light by the helmsman's hand on my shoulder.

'See de islan' dere,' the man said laconically,

gesturing towards the horizon a few degrees off the schooner's heaving bow.

I sat upright on my fragment of tarpaulin and looked where the man had pointed. The wind had freshened during the night and the horizon was veiled by a thin curtain of rain. Then through the rain, balanced on the fine thread of the horizon, I saw once again the saddle-backed silhouette of Angelina.

We drew closer, the rain cleared and the light of the rising sun gave substance to the soft-edged outline of the island. On the hillsides, I could see that the green cloak of the rain forest was embroidered with bright tongues of scarlet flame wherever the stands of immortelle and poinciana were in flower. There were few beaches: almost everywhere, the land fell steeply to the sea. The blue water seemed to break directly against the pitted limestone cliffs. The sunlight was caught by the white face of the cliffs and by the raindrops on the leaves of the trees: the island shimmered in its setting like some precious, verdant jewel.

I walked forward to the schooner's bowsprit, clutching the forestay to steady myself against the vessel's movement in the rising sea. Above me, level with the ragged birgee at the masthead, a pair of brown pelicans were making for the island on the same stiff breeze that filled the schooner's sails. Beneath the keel, the opaque blue of the open sea imperceptibly gave place to more subtle shades of blue and green as the water shoaled.

The wind began to shift into the north. The captain rose from his bed on the roof of the galley and gave a brisk order. The mainsail was close hauled and the jib reined in. Then the changing wind carried down to us the fragrance of the little island, that blend of flowers and fallen leaves and salt-stained coral rock. I filled my lungs. Instantly, tumbling down the corridor of the years, the scent of the island brought back to me the memory of that abortive visit with my father when I was a boy. I could remember how my disappointment, when the fishing boat turned south in pursuit of the tuna, had blighted all the remainder of that distant day.

The man at the wheel must have been watching my face.

'Yuh travel dere before now?' he inquired.

I shook my head. 'I came once for the fishing,' I said. 'I never stepped ashore. The tuna did not stay...'

'Yuh come for de fishin' dis time again?'

'No,' I said. 'This time it is for something else...'

The man turned his attention to the task of guiding the schooner through the maze of coral heads which broke the surface of the water all around us. In the distance, I could make out the sheltered anchorage and, at the back of it, the palm-thatched buildings of the island's only village. As we drew nearer, I could see a central square hedged about with hibiscus and yellow alamanda. From the centre of the square, the smooth grey trunk of a royal palm reached up towards the morning sky, bursting at the top into a green circlet of feathery leaves.

Set close about the square were the houses that made up the little village, each with its own small, chaotic garden of vegetables and flowers planted side by side.

Immediately behind the village rose the taller of the twin hills of the saddle-back, and I could see that a road led from the village to the summit of the hill. The road had been paved with broken coral and, in the clear morning light, its even coils glowed white against the green hillside.

The harbour was fenced off from the open sea by the inflected arms of a coral reef. There was a single, natural passage through the coral, just wide enough to admit the schooner's modest beam. The rare ships of larger size which occasionally visited the island were obliged to anchor in the open water among the coral heads.

We slipped through the passage in the coral and tied up to a wooden jetty which projected a short distance into the harbour. The cargo of smoked crevalle and the sacks of copra, for which the vessel had come, were stacked upon the jetty waiting to be loaded for the return journey. I noticed that the schooner had brought nothing to the island, as if nothing from the outside was needed there.

I took my leave of the captain.

The man said: 'If you want, when I come again next month I can return you to Cabrera. The cacique in the village, he will know when to expect me.'

I shook my head. 'I don't plan to stay until next month,' I said. 'If I can find another vessel I will be gone by the time you get back here.'

I swung my suitcase on to the jetty. The crew had already begun the task of loading the cargo into the empty hold. I knew that they intended to sail again for Port Cabrera before nightfall. They were Manzanillans, and Angelina held no attractions for them. All Angelinos, the helmsman had informed me, were simple like children. It was because there were so few of them and they bred only with each other. They lived in a world without electricity: they had never seen a motor car. They had no money to speak of, and they scarcely seemed to want any except to buy fishing line and hooks. You couldn't buy their women, so there was no profit in staying overnight.

'Dey-all is an Indian people,' the man had said, 'Dey is not like us, an' dey don' behave like udder people. It is like dey don' see no need to progress...'

He had spat over the schooner's gunwale as he spoke, to show the degree of his distaste.

He searched for words to describe his contempt. 'It is like dey satisfy wid just how dey stay,' he said at last.

CHAPTER IV

At the top of the square there was a small clapboard building with an awning of coconut branches which reached out from three of the four sides. The building evidently served as a shop, and a number of plain wooden tables had been set down beneath the awning. In place of chairs, short lengths of palm trunk had been planted upright in the packed earth of the floor around each table. Nailed to one of the mahogany pillars which supported the awning, there was a hand lettered sign which read: *Altara Anandara*, and immediately below: *Cacique of Angelina*.

I walked between the empty tables and into the shop. It was cool inside and dark. After the harsh early morning glare reflected from the water in the harbour, my eyes took a moment to adjust to the soft light. The shop smelt of salt fish and hemp rope and coconut oil. An ancient ship's lantern, still mounted in its brass gimbals, hung from a beam in the ceiling. Behind the mahogany counter, worn smooth by generations of daily use, a man was arranging coils of fishing line on a shelf. He turned to look at me as I approached the counter. I put my case down on the floor and introduced myself. The man made a grave, old fashioned bow, a coil of line still clutched in one large hand.

'My name is Altara Anandara,' he announced in that soft, precise, curiously accented English which I soon discovered was spoken by all Angelinos. 'I am cacique of Angelina.'

My back ached from my night on the unyielding planks of the schooner's deck. 'They gave me your name in Manzanilla,' I said. 'I am here for a few days. I need to rent a place to stay.'

In the half light of the shop, we took a closer look at each other. Across the wooden counter, I saw a man of late middle age with high cheek bones and weathered, light brown skin. His straight black hair was marked with grey, not at the temples but in a broad, even swathe backwards from the centre of his hairline. His eyes were set deep in their sockets and the lantern above cast them in shadow.

The cacique, I realised, would have seen a very different individual: a white man some years younger than himself, who had not shaved for two days, whose clothes were creased and stained from travel, and whose general state of mind was no doubt mirrored in his own eyes.

'I put first things first,' the cacique said quietly. 'I welcome you to Angelina. We do not have many visitors to our island.'

He looked down at the coil of line in his hand and put it on the counter.

'It is true I have a small place which visitors can

rent. It has two rooms and there is a latrine at the back. I do not know if it would please you.'

I was suddenly very tired. 'If it has a roof and a bed I will take it,' I said.

The cacique said: 'Then let us go there now...'

He led the way out of the shop to an open yard at the back. In the shade of a silk cotton tree, a donkey slept lightly between the shafts of a high-slung cart. The cacique loaded my case on to a platform at the back.

'You can get up,' he said.

I took my place on the bench seat. The cacique got up beside me and shook the reins. The donkey leant into the harness and we began the journey. We passed slowly along the unpaved main street of the village: the donkey's delicate hooves raised a little cloud of dust in our wake. Two black and white goats and a flock of foraging chickens reluctantly gave way to the cart and its passengers.

The women of the village were at work in their gardens and in the open yards behind their huts. Although it was still early morning, they were already beginning to prepare their family's evening meal. Breadfruit and hands of green bananas were simmering over charcoal fires. Their children played together at the front of the huts and spilled over into the empty roadway in laughing, chattering groups. No one wore shoes, and I saw that their clothes had been patched and patched again; but like the little huts in which they lived, they did not look neglected.

I saw that the helmsman had been right: they were an Indian people, and they shared a startling family resemblance, with exactly the same high cheek bones and fine, deep-set eyes as their cacique. As we passed by, the women and children stopped what they had been doing to inspect me. A little girl waved both hands and a woman called out in English: 'You welcome here.' The shy greeting was echoed by others as we passed.

The cacique said: 'We not see many visitors in Angelina. They are happy you will stay with us...'

I raised my hand awkwardly to return their greetings. 'Where are the men?' I asked.

'All the men at sea,' the cacique said. 'They leave before sun up...'

They left at first light every morning, he explained. They needed to make use of the early morning off-shore breeze to carry them to the fishing banks to the east beyond the sight of land. They travelled together and the catch belonged equally to them all. It was shared out when they returned at the end of the day: the fish that were more than the people could eat were smoked the next morning and would be sent to Manzanilla when the time came. That, and the sacks of copra I had seen on the jetty, earned them the money to buy from outside their island the few things they could not make themselves.

At the edge of the village, we passed a small building with split coconut trunk walls and a shingled roof. It lay within a circle of queen conch shells, their apices planted firmly in the soil. I asked what the building was for and the cacique halted the cart for a moment to show me. 'It is our clinic,' he said proudly. 'Before, our people had no place to stay when they were sick.'

The cart passed out of the village. The coral road,

whose steep white coils I had seen from the deck of the schooner, lay ahead of us.

'Now we must walk,' the cacique announced. 'The donkey can carry only the baggage up this hill.'

I climbed down from my seat and fell in beside the cacique at the back of the cart. The road swung sharply to the right: the donkey slowed its pace and began the climb.

We climbed together in comfortable silence. From time to time, breathing heavily behind the cart, I looked out through gaps in the screen of trees towards the southern horizon. Manzanilla, I knew, lay not far beyond it. It was a distance, I thought, that could not be measured in miles.

Everywhere about us on the hill, the rainforest threatened to take back what it had given up to the spades and cutlasses which had fashioned the road. The narrow coils of packed coral were narrowed again by the advance of flowering vines and resurgent undergrowth. At one hairpin bend where the donkey stopped of its own accord to rest, a vast stand of balasier with scarlet, boat-shaped bracts, overhung the road almost to its crown. A barrel-trunked guango tree, its branches bearded with epiphytes, cast its great shadow across the road. Within the forest itself, the dark soil gave rise to a wild profusion of growth. I could see that many trees were bound to each other by lianas as thick as my arm: they hung down in grey-green loops to the rich earth.

The donkey stopped for the second time when we were halfway up the hill. A pair of pierid butterflies, attracted by the rivulets of sweat, settled on the animal's flank. The metallic scent of fallen hog plums was heavy on the air. As I stood for a moment in the shade of the plum tree, the silence around us was broken by the call of a mountain whistler. The shy bird's song was a series of clear whistles in phrases of two or three crystal notes, dropping more than an octave on the scale. The donkey, suddenly impatient to move on, stamped its hooves sharply on the roadway. The whistling song was abandoned in mid-phrase. I caught a brief glimpse of pearl grey wings as the bird took flight. At once, the silence of the forest flowed back beneath the canopy of the leaves. The cacique slapped the donkey lightly on the rump. We moved on.

Just below the summit of the hill, the donkey stopped for the third time. I wiped the sweat from my eyes with the back of my hand. The cacique leant for a moment against the side of the cart. Directly below us, I could see the casually laid out huts of the village. I realised for the first time that, apart from what I had learnt on the schooner, I knew nothing about the people who owned them.

'How many people live on Angelina?' I asked.

The cacique took a moment to consider the figure. 'We are three hundred and ninety,' he said at last; then he corrected himself. 'Three hundred and ninety one. We were given a boy last night. I have already entered the name in my register...'

'And how many white people?'

'Now you have come,' he said, 'there are four.'

I wiped the sweat from my eyes again, conscious of

how unfit I had allowed myself to become.

'And who are the others?' I asked.

The donkey reached out towards a stand of grass at the edge of the road: the cart began to drift backwards. The cacique checked its movement with his foot.

'First,' he said slowly, giving thought to how best he could describe the three people of my own colour who had settled among them, 'first there is Pra Latana. His given name is O'Malloran and we have heard once he was a priest. We call him Pra Latana; it means 'the one who understands us.' He has learnt our language. It is not a thing easily done, so we think perhaps he loves us.'

The unexpected mention of a man who might have been a priest reminded me of something I had noticed as we passed through the village: there was no church among the little houses, not even a modest wooden chapel. I asked why.

The cacique pushed his high-crowned straw hat to the back of his head.

'They say we are a simple people, and it is true,' he said quietly. 'Before memory began we carried our own faith to this island. We do not seek it in a building. In the time of our ancestors, Spanish came in their ships from Manzanilla to raise a church here for our village; but none of our people wished for a church. It is not our way. When the Spanish left, we removed the building. You can see where it stood near the palm tree in the square. Our ancestors meant no disrespect, but it was not our way.'

He spread the fingers of both hands in a curious, open gesture.

'Pra Latana understands our way,' he said.

I knew that the Spanish Jesuits who followed the conquistadores had not been scrupulous about the methods they employed to persuade the people of the New World to their own belief. I thought it would have taken a brave people to resist them.

'And the others?' I asked.

'There is Mr Brucknor,' the cacique said. 'He has a little house by the sea. When he came to Angelina he brought a servant from Haiti to look after him. They live there together in the house.'

'What does Mr Brucknor do?' I asked.

The cacique considered this for a moment. 'In truth he does little,' he admitted. 'But he is no longer a young man. He owns many books, they fill his house and he reads them all the time. He must know many things, but he is a private man and he does not speak much about himself. We do not feel we know him well because he keeps his distance from us.'

'And the third one?' I asked. 'You said there were three men.'

The cacique laughed softly at my mistake. 'Ah, that man is a lady,' he said in his precise way. 'That is Miss Katy. We think of her as one of us, for she was born here on Angelina.'

He stepped back a few yards on the dusty road and pointed down through a break in the trees to a sprawling, shingled house set on a green spit of land above an arc of coral beach.

'Miss Katy lives there,' he said. 'The house was built by her grandfather. When I was a boy myself, the family used to visit from Manzanilla every year after the hurricane season had come and gone. Sometimes they would stay two, three months; now Miss Katy stays with us all year round.'

He took off his high-crowned hat and wiped the sweat from his temples.

'We were born the same month, Miss Katy and me. We have known each other from our beginnings. She is part of us here on Angelina. We are happy she is pleased to grow old amongst us.'

I was curious to know something about his own position on the island.

'Who appointed you cacique?' I asked.

'From before memory began, there has been a cacique on Angelina. He is chosen by our people. After Manzanilla took its independence, the governor on Grand Trinity came to tell us that he would look after us. He visits once each year…'

He spread the fingers of both hands again.

'He tells me that I should represent him on the island. I keep the registers for him and he gives me a chain to hang around my neck. It has a silver label on it which says 'Cacique'. He thinks I wear it every day,' he confided, 'but in truth I only use it when he comes to see us.'

He laughed softly at the thought of this small deception.

'Now they wish to take us all to live on Grand Trinity,' he said, no longer smiling. 'The governor says they would build good houses for us with water and electric light, and our lives would be better. But we could never leave our island, so we have stayed as we are. I asked the governor to help us build a clinic, but he was vexed because we would not leave and nothing was built. Then Pra Latana came to us...'

He rapped the side of the cart with his open hand; the donkey leant into the harness and we moved forward again.

It took another five minutes to complete the climb to the top of the hill. My case was heavy and I understood why the cacique had decided to bring it up in the cart. Then we emerged from the shade of the overhanging trees on to a narrow grassy plateau. The paraa grass shimmered in the fierce heat of the morning sun. I looked at the cacique who had removed his hat again. The fine coral dust, thrown up by the donkey's hooves, had caked thickly on his brown face. Broad rivulets of sweat ran down his forehead carving their way through the white mask of dust in a pattern of vertical stripes.

He noticed me looking at him. 'Yes I am striped like the tiger,' he said suddenly. 'I have seen pictures of the jungle...' He rested his hands on his hips and his body shook with laughter like a child at the simple thought of it.

The bungalow I had rented stood at one edge of the little plateau. It was as the cacique had described it: a simple rectangular structure divided by a screen of coconut matting into two rooms of equal size. The walls were made of limestone blocks fitted together without mortar. The high-pitched roof was thatched with coconut boughs. There were wooden shutters at the windows, but no glazing. An open veranda ran the full length of all four sides and split-bamboo guttering hung beneath the eaves to catch the rainwater and lead it into a tank set on a platform beneath a cinnamon tree. At the rear of the building, joined to it by a covered walkway, there was a kitchen whose walls were fashioned from the bud shields of a royal palm. From behind the kitchen, a gravelled path led to a pit latrine set among the trees at the edge of the plateau.

I inspected the house with its owner. I would need someone to cook for me and to wash my clothes. The cacique had already considered it.

'I can send someone to mind you,' he said. 'I will ask her to meet you here in the morning. You can tell her what you like to eat. You will need kerosene for the lamp...'

'Open an account for me,' I said, 'I will settle with you when I leave.'

I asked about the weekly rental of the house. The cacique named a figure which was less than I had paid the captain of the schooner for the use of his cabin for a single night.

'I think you should ask more,' I said.

He shook his head. 'It is what I charge,' he said simply.

He carried my case into the house, returned to the cart and took up the reins in his large hands.

'I will send my son to you this evening with food,' he said. 'The girl will come in the morning. I wish you an easeful day.'

Then he raised his hand in grave salute, flicked the

reins and started down the hill. I watched until the cart and its driver had passed out of sight. For several minutes after that, I could follow its progress through the trees by the high-pitched squeal of the wooden brake shoe as it chafed against its wheel. An easeful day, I thought, was pretty much what I had hoped to find on Angelina.

I walked around the side of the house to the water tank. At its base there was a heavy brass spigot. I turned it on. The water gushed from the spout in a quicksilver stream; then it broke and raced across the hard earth in a hundred separate, glittering rivulets of light. I shut off the flow. There was a hinged lid set into the cedar cover of the tank with a copper ladle beside it. I raised the lid, picked up the ladle: the water was cool on my tongue and smelt of cinnamon. I wiped my mouth with the back of my hand and went into the house to escape the sun.

The bungalow was furnished with unpolished mahogany furniture, heavy and durable like the rough-hewn blocks that made up the walls. The planks of the floor were covered in places with strips of coconut matting. In the centre of the first room, there was a table with four chairs around it and a brass kerosene lamp set down on a mat in the middle of the table. There was a cupboard in the corner and two shelves had been let into the whitewashed walls. I pulled aside a matting screen and walked into the second room. It contained a plain cedar bedstead with a clean mattress and a blanket folded neatly at the foot. I pressed down on the mattress with my hand: like the mattress I had always slept on at

Sans Souci, it was stuffed with shredded coconut fibre. In front of the open window there was a washstand with a red clay ewer and basin, and a bar of red carbolic soap in a clay dish beside the ewer.

I went outside to the kitchen. On a wooden rack fixed to one of the corner posts I found plates and cutlery. Two metal saucepans hung from nails driven into a cross beam above my head. A clay coalpot stood on a platform on the floor with a sack of charcoal beside it. On a shelf in the corner, a ripe hand of bananas lay in a shallow woven basket; the bunch from which it had been cut was suspended from a metal hook screwed into one of the rafters. The bananas were firm and sweet.

The kitchen lay in the shadow of an ancient guango tree. The reptilian roots snaked across the bare earth and then plunged down towards the heart of the island, The branches of the tree were bearded with epiphytes: the largest had produced a cluster of blood red blossoms with pointed, waxy sepals. From the hollow angle each branch made with the trunk, tendrils of the night-blooming cereus hung down towards the earth. The plain white buds were shut tight against the daylight, their exquisite fragrance securely locked away until darkness prised them open to flower briefly and unseen during the course of the night. There had been a night-blooming cereus in the branches of the old poinciana tree in the garden at Sans Souci and, though I never saw the open flower, the sweet scent had sometimes drifted through the window of my bedroom before I fell asleep.

At the front of the bungalow there had been a brave

attempt to lay out a flower garden in four small squares, each separated by a narrow interval of coarse gravel. The sun, the rain and the richness of the dark earth had combined to frustrate the cacique's ordered plan. The flowering plants, which should have confined themselves to their appointed beds, had burst out of these natural boundaries and swept across the level ground and down the slope of the hillside. In the gaps between the trees at the edge of the rainforest, there were now broad stands of yellow alamanda and hastate ginger lilies.

I looked out over the tangled mass of colour to the sea. The wind had risen since the schooner docked: the water beyond the inflected arms of the little harbour was veined with white. Somewhere in the branches further down the hill, the mountain whistler resumed its interrupted song. Without warning, I felt my heart race and the muscles of my throat constrict. An image of Justine came flooding into my mind. It was summer in England, the window of the cottage we had rented was open and she lay asleep upon her stomach on the bed. Her long legs were spread wide so that I could see the sweet pinkness there in the secret cleft of her body. There had been birdsong in the tree outside the window, and then, as now, I had felt myself consumed by an almost unendurable longing for her.

Scarcely aware of what I was doing, I seized my case from the bedroom where the cacique had left it and began to hurry down the hill, back towards the village and the schooner in the harbour. If I caught the vessel in time I could be in Port Cabrera again next day and back in London, perhaps, the day after that. I could wait for her in the flat, as I had done before, until she tired of Luis and Madeira and came home.

The case was heavy and the metal handle, which had long ago shed its leather sheath, bit into the palm of my hand. I did not notice the discomfort. At the hairpin bend where the donkey had stopped to rest, there was a break in the trees through which I had been able to see the harbour. As I looked now, the schooner with its mainsail set passed through the narrow exit and into the open sea. I could make out the captain gesticulating on the fo'c'sle, finding some fault with the way the crew had stacked the sacks of copra on the deck.

I released my grip on the case: it fell, in the dust of the roadway. I wanted to wave my arms and yell at the top of my voice, but I knew that against the background of the forest no one on the vessel would see me.

I sat down at the edge of the road to recover my breath. An iridescent ground lizard emerged from the undergrowth, took careful note of me and raced across to the opposite side. After a while, I took hold of the case again and retraced my steps back up the hill. I was aware this time of the weight of the case and of the edge of the metal handle biting into the flesh of my palm. It took a long time to regain the summit of the hill and the refuge of my bungalow.

Towards sunset, the cacique's son brought me a meal. The boy carried the food in one of those old fashioned enamel carriers, which had always reminded me of the pictures I had seen of Chinese pagodas. At Sans Souci, the overseers used to hang them from their saddles when they planned to spend the day in the fields. Whenever I passed by on my donkey, they would offer to share with me the contents of the three containers clipped one above the other into the framework of the handle. Some of them, I remembered, also carried with them a hip flask of spirits which they produced from their saddle bags with a conspiratorial wink whenever my father was out of sight.

'For de rheumatism, young baas,' they would say as they held the flask to their lips. It was hot in the fields at Sans Souci when the breeze failed, and the days were long.

The cacique's son had brought with him a half bottle of white rum. I saw that it was the same Manzanillan brand that my father used to drink, with the familiar picture of a sugar factory on the label. The boy had also brought a tin container filled with kerosene for the lamp. He laid the carrier and the rum together on the kitchen table and put the kerosene down on the packed-earth floor.

I thanked him and reached into my pocket for some copper coins I had carried with me from Manzanilla. He smiled shyly and shook his head.

'There is no need,' he said quietly.

I watched his slight figure until it had passed out of sight on its way back down the hill. I fetched a glass from the kitchen and opened the bottle of rum. The fierce, oily spirit seared my throat. Recalling how the overseers always did it, I chased the drink with water from the tank outside; then I refilled my glass from the bottle.

I sat out on the veranda to eat my meal. The boy had brought lobster in one of the square containers and, in the others, there was yam and sweet potato and pale slices of christophine in a pale sauce.

When I had finished eating, I sat back in my chair and looked out over the island. Purple shadows had settled in the hollows of the hillside and I could sense that the tropical night was gathering itself to fall upon the place all in one piece like a shutter. From somewhere in the village at the foot of the hill, the donkey brayed. A bat passed across the evening sky, the translucent wings briefly silhouetted against the last bright flourish of the sunset.

The rum failed to bring me comfort, but this time I felt sure that it was something more than my longing for Justine. I tried unsuccessfully to give it form. I could say for certain only that it grew from a wider sense of failure – a dissatisfaction with the whole course of my adult life. I had chosen to be a journalist; I knew that I was good at my job and careful of the quality of my work. But, unlike some of my colleagues, I had never believed that what I did really affected the actions of other people. I did not deceive myself. My regular columns were like the flowers of the tree hibiscus – born at first light, fallen to earth by nightfall. I could remember once, on that first occasion when Justine had gone away, how I had walked out one evening to buy myself a meal of fish and chips. As I ate the meal at the kitchen table I saw that the food had been wrapped in the page of the newspaper which carried my column of the previous day. The grease from the wilting chips had saturated the paper and, beneath the heading which carried my name, the words had disappeared in a yellow, oily stain. It was as if they had never been written.

Later that night, after the last of the rum had gone, I groped my way in the darkness to my bed and covered myself with the blanket against the cool night air. My sleep was broken during the night by the cry of an owl, a bitter sense of my own inadequacy and an aching hunger for the touch of my wife.

CHAPTER V

I woke early. A shaft of sunlight entered through the unshuttered window and fell across my face. The diamond light scored my eyes. Little motes of dust floated weightless in the shaft of light. On the grass outside, a pair of grey-winged doves were feeding in the long shadow of the guango tree. I recognised the plaintive, low-keyed call of the male bird.

I wrapped a towel round my waist and stepped on to the veranda at the back of the house. A short distance away, there was a pool of water. Directly above me, a single cloud had been touched by the light of the morning sun. The scarlet image of the cloud hung in the depths of the pool, more beautiful than the cloud itself.

I dressed and rummaged in my case. Beneath the picture of Justine, I found my sketch pad. I sat beside the reeds at the edge of the pool and sought to capture the reflection of the cloud in the water. The image was pierced by the hastate buds of a water lily. After a while, defeated by the subtlety of the shifting reflections in the water, I gave up. The sketch pad slipped from my knee.

A long-tailed ground lizard, which had approached me as I worked, fled into the grass.

I heard footsteps on the gravelled path at the front of the bungalow. I got up and walked round the side of the building. A girl stood on the path that led to the front steps. She had long dark hair caught by a ribbon at the nape of her neck and she was dressed in a short skirt and the kind of loose, sleeveless blouse worn by all the women I had seen in the village the previous day. Like theirs, her feet were bare: the pale brown skin was mottled by the coral dust of the roadway.

The girl looked up as I approached.

'Good day,' she said gravely, with that soft, precise intonation I had noticed in the cacique and his son. 'My name is Apparani. The cacique send me to you.'

I considered for a moment. 'Well, Apparani,' I said, 'I need someone to cook for me and wash my clothes for a few days while I am here. Will you do that?'

'I will do it,' the girl replied. 'You must tell me only what you wish to eat.'

I realised that since the day Justine left I had given no thought at all to what I ate. I had taken no pleasure from any of my meals. With an effort, I forced myself to give the girl a considered answer. I thought of what we had eaten at Sans Souci when I was a boy.

'I like jack crevalle and lobster,' I said slowly, 'and sweet potatoes and yam and okra soup and rock crab and plantain.'

The girl listened carefully. 'I can cook all that for you,' she said simply.

'Buy what you need from the cacique's shop,' I told her. 'I have spoken to him.'

She nodded. 'He has told me,' she said.

She went round the back to inspect the kitchen. I listened to her rinsing the saucepans beneath the brass tap I had tested. After a while, I heard her steps on the gravel path again and I watched as she started down the hill to find my food.

I went back to my chair at the edge of the water and recovered my sketch pad from the grass. But that first raw explosion of colour had already faded from the morning sky and the single cloud had drifted from its place above the pool. I looked without satisfaction at what I had drawn; then thinking of the Indian girl's loose-limbed grace as she walked along the gravel path, I wondered whether I could at least still draw the human figure.

When we were first married, I used to sketch Justine. She would pose naked for me, proud of her slim-waisted beauty – and secretly contemptuous, as I think now, of how I had allowed it to enslave me.

After a while, she had become bored with sitting for me, just as she became bored sooner or later with most things that once amused her. So I had put away my sketch pad and, not long afterwards, she had left me for the first time. Later, when she came back, I did not suggest that she should sit for me again.

At midday, I had a second visitor. There were footsteps at the front of the house and I heard a man call my name.

I went to the open door. A tall white man dressed in an ancient safari jacket and stained white trousers stood on the wooden steps. He was a man of late middle age and, in spite of his threadbare clothes, he carried himself with a certain confident grace. He brought his heels together as I approached and bowed slightly from the waist. There was a faint, incongruous whiff of bay rum on the still morning air.

'You must forgive me for arriving so early in the day,' the man said, 'but I wanted to be the first to welcome you to Angelina.' He spoke with a slight accent which I couldn't place. 'I learnt from the cacique you had arrived. I hope you will let me know if I can be of assistance in any way while you are here. As you will discover, the island lacks certain advantages...'

I said: 'I think I passed your clinic on my way...'

The man laughed and held up his hand to stop me going further.

'You mistake me for Father O'Malloran,' he said. 'He is the other one. My name is Brucknor and I am sorry to say that, unlike his, my own charitable instincts died many years ago.'

I said that the cacique had spoken of him. 'I do not have much to do with the Angelinos,' he said. 'They are not an educated people and the truth is we have little to say to each other. We tend to remain in our separate worlds.'

He removed his hat and wiped his forehead with a faded silk handkerchief. 'I came to say that I hope one evening you will come to dinner with me. Unlike Miss Katy, I do not have the benefit of a generator and electric light but I have learnt that kerosene lanterns have a certain charm. Perhaps you will allow me to suggest a date a little later in your stay…'

He bowed slightly from the waist again. 'You will need time to yourself this first day,' he said. 'I wish you an agreeable stay on this island.'

He replaced his sweat-stained hat and I watched his shabby, elegant figure as he started back through the trees on the narrow path by which he had arrived. The faint smell of the astringent bay rum hung about the steps of the bungalow for several minutes after he had gone.

Apparani returned from the village, a wicker basket balanced effortlessly on her head. She set the basket down for my inspection. Laid out with unconscious artistry on a green banana leaf were the elements of my next meal. In the centre of the leaf there was a jack crevalle and, beside the glistening silver fish, a Negro yam still wrapped in its fibrous jacket, three sweet potatoes, an ear of corn, a breadfruit and a pair of okras for my soup.

I thanked her and the girl carried the basket into the kitchen and prepared to light a fire in the coal pot.

For the second time that morning, I took up my sketch pad and pastels. I walked out to the edge of the grassy plateau. Through a break in the trees, I looked down on the blue harbour water beyond the thatched roofs of the village. I sat crossed-legged on the grass. After a while, the movement of my hand across the paper became more assured. The outline of the village below me began to take shape.

An hour later, the girl came out to tell me that my

meal was ready. I heard behind me the sharp intake of her breath as she caught sight of what I had done. I held the pad out at arms length to have a better look at the sketch. At once I could see the fault that spoiled it: the perspective was untrue. It was the old weakness which I had never learnt to correct.

'I haven't caught the colour of the water,' I said out loud, pretending it was a fault I could put right. I took up my pen to cross the picture through. As I did so, the girl stepped forward and pointed shyly at one of the thatched huts at the edge of the village. 'I see my father's house,' she said. 'You have drawn our yard.'

I tore the page from the pad and rolled it into a cylinder. 'You can have it if you like,' I said. She took it carefully from me as if it was something of value, and I wished as I gave it to her that I had taken more trouble with the outline of the place where she lived.

Later in the afternoon, I took the blanket from my bedroom and laid it on the grass beneath the guango tree at the back of the bungalow. I slept in the shade beneath the branches of the tree. When I woke, it was already getting dark and the girl had prepared my evening meal.

'There is no need for you to stay now.' I said.

She extinguished the coalpot fire and said goodnight.

'Ask the cacique,' I said, 'to let me know when the next schooner is expected to call, I want him to arrange for me to return to Manzanilla.'

'I will do it,' Apparani said. 'And when I come tomorrow I will wash your clothes...'

From the veranda of the bungalow I saw her set off down the hill in the gathering darkness, the cylinder of paper grasped firmly in her hand.

I ate my meal, undressed and lay on the bed. The whistling melody of the tree frogs in the branches of the guango filled the dark room with sound. Above my head, the white cedar joists contracted with sharp movements in the cool night air. I suddenly wished that I was staying on just long enough to draw the girl. I would use charcoal on cream paper. I would draw her walking first, with that loose-limbed grace; then I would draw her face with its startling cheek-bones. I had noticed how her dark eyes were tilted upwards at the corners...

It was with the image of the girl's face on my mind that I fell asleep without pulling the blanket over my body. My dreams, however, were all of Justine and Luis who did not know me when I approached them in the cobbled Madeiran street.

CHAPTER VI

When I woke up on the morning of my third day on Angelina, the girl was already there. I could hear her singing softly to herself as she worked. She had a clear, sweet voice and she sang in the language of her people. I got out of bed, pushed aside the screen of coconut matting and walked into the other room. Apparani brought her hands together in greeting and said: 'The cacique send to say the next schooner is not for some days yet. Since you wish to return to Manzanilla, he will arrange it at that time. He sorry you wish to leave us so soon.'

I sat down heavily at the table and wondered how I was going to pass the unwanted days before I could start home again. Apparani brought in a tray with casava bread and a star apple sliced in half. I suddenly thought how foolish I had been to travel on to Angelina. I was filled with fear that Justine might have tired of Luis and would already be on her way back to London. She would return to our flat and find it deserted. I had left no note. Always in the past I had waited for her: she had always known that I would be there when she came back. That knowledge was her rock she used to say; the one firm point in the compass of her life.

The fear took away my appetite: I forced myself to eat a little of the casava. In order to make my remaining days on Angelina pass more quickly, I knew that I would have to occupy my time with more than my fears. The cacique had spoken of a footpath which followed the contours of the island's coastline and linked each small settlement along the way to the village and its harbour. I finished my meal and set off down the hill. At the place where I had dismounted from the cart, the footpath branched away to the east. I followed it.

The path ran along the top of the cliffs, which had been undercut at their base by the action of the waves. The prevailing wind drove a long swell against the undercut face of the cliff. The ancient limestone rock was honeycombed with vertical shafts that led down from the top of the cliffs to the sea. From time to time a geyser of water, forced upwards by the weight of a wave far below, would burst into the sunlight from the mouth of a fissure beside the path. I could taste the salt in the air. Salt water rainbows took form, hung for a moment in the air above my head and then dissolved as I reached out towards them.

The trees of the rainforest had kept their distance from the sea. The coastal path ran down the centre of a broad strip of scrubland which separated the forest from the cliffs. At one side of the path there was a shallow expanse of fresh water. A solitary purple gaulin stood on one leg among the lily pads, its eyes closed firmly against the diamond light. The bird ignored me as I passed by.

At intervals along the coast, the sea had carved little horseshoe bays into the limestone fabric of the island. The path would descend abruptly from the cliffs to a crescent of bright coral sand studded with sea grape and groves of coconut palms. At some of these places, there were two or three thatched huts raised up from the sand on wooden stilts among the palms. On the slope of the hillside at the back of the huts I could see that space had been opened in the green wall of the forest for beds of yam and sweet potato and the other once familiar vegetables of my childhood. The women and children of the settlements were weeding among the raised beds; I could hear the voices of the children as they worked.

At the top of the sand in each bay, beyond the reach of the next high water, there was a collection of wooden rollers on which the canoes had been launched at first light and which would be used again to recover them when they returned from the banks in the evening. In the intervals between the huts, older canoes had been drawn out of the water for repair. They lay upturned on the sand, waiting for their lives to be renewed with boiling tar and oakum.

Except for a few old grandfathers, the island had been left in the care of its women and children when the men sailed out on the morning breeze. Those I passed on the way offered grave, old fashioned courtesies and wished me well. One, a little bolder than the rest, asked me how long I planned to stay with them. I found I could not say, 'Only as long as I have to,' so I lied and claimed I did not know.

The cliffs grew taller as I walked on. In places the ancient limestone had been eroded into fantastic leonine shapes by the wind and the scouring action of the salt spray thrown up by the waves. A scarlet flower whose name I had forgotten sprang from the thin overlay of the soil and decorated the cliff tops with unexpected bursts of colour.

I looked more closely at the huts I passed. They were all built to a common pattern, propped up on six arthritic legs which raised them a convenient distance off the bare sand around them. Where the overlapping planks had rotted through, the holes were neatly patched with the tops and bottoms of discarded kerosene tins. On some of the rusting metal squares, the name of the original owner was legible still: 'Standard Oil Company of New Jersey' I read: 'This end up'. On either side of the wooden steps that led up to the front doors, coralita vines had scaled the walls as high as the grass-thatched roofs. The massed pink flowers, which clustered everywhere along the convoluted vines, softened the bare outlines of the little huts. A child waved at me. I raised my own hand awkwardly in response.

I had been walking for more than an hour and a half when the footpath changed direction. It swung abruptly to the west, drawing me along the southern shore and back in towards the village. The cliffs were not as high on this side of the island and, because the shoreline was shielded from the force of the waves by a broad ribbon of coral reef, the base of the cliff had not been undercut by the sea. The contours of the reef matched exactly those of the shoreline, so the ribbon of coral remained at an even distance from the land all along its length. The narrow channel in between was like a river open at both ends: the afternoon sun struck shifting patterns of light in the flow of green water.

The heat distorted the light on the path ahead of me. A weathered coral boulder at the side of the path quivered in the heat. The path fell away abruptly to another horseshoe bay. A group of children were collecting green coconuts from a tree close to the water's edge. The oldest boy had climbed the vertical trunk with practised ease; he was twisting the nuts from their holdfast beneath the branches. The younger children were gathering the fallen nuts and tying them in pairs by the flexible cords which had attached them to the tree. The boy in the tree caught sight of me before the others. He slid down the trunk and landed lightly on the loose sand. He took up his cutlass, laid open one of the nuts and held it out to me. The water was sweet and cool on my tongue. I thanked the boy and walked on. Behind me, the children abandoned their work and flung themselves into the water. The oldest boy hauled himself on to a ledge in the face of the cliff and then plunged into the sea. The brief fountain of spray was jewelled by the sunlight. The laughter of the children playing in the water followed me along the path which sloped upwards again to the top of the cliff.

It took another hour before I found myself at the bottom of the south side of the hill on which my house stood. The village was a short distance ahead of me: my circuit was almost complete. The footpath climbed over a headland of honeycombed rock. On the far side of the headland there was one last bay set deep into the face of the cliff. The muscles of my thighs ached from the unaccustomed effort of my walk. I rested for a moment against the fallen trunk of a white cedar tree. A pair of pale pink flowers showed that the tree still clung to life by a thin sheaf of roots which had survived its fall.

The mouth of the bay was drawn in sharply by two rocky arms which reached out towards each other from the cliff face on either side. It reminded me of one of those swollen green glass demi-johns with narrow necks in which the shop keepers of Port Cabrera used to store their rum. At its broadest point, the bay was no more than a hundred yards wide. In the centre a single stand of stags horn coral pierced the surface of the water as the tide ran out. On the beach, an uneven crescent of shells and sargasso weed marked the limit of the last high water. Except for the soft gasp of the waves and the occasional fencing of the ghost crabs in the weed, there was silence all around me. Almost against my will, my thoughts turned back again to that sterile strip of sand which had usurped the place of the beach I had loved at Sans Souci.

There was a dinghy tethered at the mouth of the bay. I could see that the little vessel was loaded to the gunwales with what appeared to be a cargo of rocks. Waist deep in the water beside it, a man was removing the rocks one at a time and laying them on top of each other on the sea floor. The rocks were large and irregular in shape, and the man worked slowly because it was not easy to lift them out of the boat from his position in the water beside it. As I watched, one of the rocks fell out of the man's grasp and into the deeper water beyond the structure he was building. He struggled for a moment to regain his footing on the sea floor; then he looked up and caught sight of me on the beach. He hailed me across the water.

'You!' I heard him shout. 'Wait there. I want to talk to you.'

I did as I was told. I was tired now my walk was coming to its end: the sweat stung my eyes and ran down from my temples to the point of my chin.

The man waded out of the sea, made fast the dinghy to a manchineel tree at the water's edge and began to clamber round the shore of the bay towards me. He clutched awkwardly at the pitted limestone to keep his balance. As he came closer, I saw that he was a large, pink, balding man of about my own age. He wore a ragged pair of swimming trunks and mismatched tennis shoes, through which the yellow joints of his toes were visible. He had not shaved recently and his eyes were red-rimmed from the glare of the sunlight on the water. He did not smile as he approached me.

'You the man who's taken the cacique's bungalow?' he demanded. 'The cacique told me you were here.'

Water dripped from the hem of his swimming trunks on to the sand.

'My name's O'Malloran,' he said.

In spite of the heat of the afternoon sun, he shivered a little as he spoke and drew his arms across his chest. I saw that the skin of his fingers was dead white and pleated like linen from being too long in the water. He pointed out towards the laden dinghy.

'I am laying down a sea wall to enclose the inlet,' he said.

I asked the obvious question.

'I am going to breed loggerheads. The females will lay there on the beach in the season. The hatchlings will be trapped in the enclosure. They will grow well there.'

I asked what he intended to do with them. The question seemed to irritate him. I could guess that he was an easily irritated man.

'Sell them, of course,' he said sharply. 'There's a market for turtle flesh in San Juan. I can sell the shells there too.'

He looked closely at me for the first time. It was clear that he wanted to explain. He made a sweeping gesture with one arm which seemed to embrace the entire island.

'Angelina needs a decent clinic and a nurse to staff it. What I can do is not enough. Last year two of our children died waiting to get to hospital on Grand Trinity. They should not have died and I couldn't help them. When I sell enough turtles, what is needed can be paid for. There must be no more deaths of that kind.'

I said: 'I thought the island was a British responsibility. Have you asked them to provide what you need?'

'I have never cared for the British,' he said, looking me in the face. 'And the British do not care for me. They have been trying for years to resettle the population on Grand Trinity. It would be more convenient for them, but they do not understand that the people would never leave. They do not listen to what I tell them, so I must raise the money myself. It will take time, but it can be done.'

I thought of the patched wooden walls of the huts I had seen and of the women and children at work in the sun while their men fished the far banks.

'Isn't it possible the people might be better off if they were resettled?' I asked. 'There doesn't seem to be much for them here.'

His body stiffened with anger. 'You have got a lot to learn,' he said brusquely.

I looked out again towards the mouth of the bay; I could just make out across the white sand of the sea floor the shadow of the rock wall the man was building there. The foundation of the structure had reached across the narrow entrance five feet beneath the surface, but I could see that the hard part remained to be done.

'Two of us could finish the job in three months,' O'Malloran said. 'A task like that needs one man in the water and another in the boat. The female turtles arrive to lay their eggs in eight weeks time. I want your help.'

He made it sound more of a demand than a request. The muscles in the small of my back ached now with a dull insistence. I struggled for a moment against the temptation of a sharp retort.

'I am only here for a few days,' I said at last. 'I am leaving on the next schooner to call.'

For a brief moment, I saw the disappointment register on the man's unattractive face.

'A bird of passage then,' he said resentfully. 'Well, in that case you are no good to me.'

The long climb up the hill to my bungalow still lay ahead of me. I was thirsty again. 'I must get on,' I said and turned to go.

'Wait,' O'Malloran said. 'I want to talk to you again. Come to my place tomorrow after work. I will give you a meal...'

I reached at once for some credible excuse, but I could think of none. Out at the entrance to the bay, I saw the tethered dinghy swing slowly round to face the first slight surge of the incoming tide.

'All right,' I heard myself answer gracelessly. 'I will come tomorrow.'

O'Malloran made fists of his large hands and knuckled his red-rimmed eyes. It was an awkward habit which would become familiar to me in the days that followed.

'Come at six,' he said, 'Anyone will show you where.'

I walked on, following the path that led up from the bay to the top of the cliff again. Ahead of me, a file of ancient divi-divi trees, their branches sculpted into flat planes by the force of the prevailing wind, marked the approach to the village. I walked past O'Malloran's clinic and began the climb up the hill to my house.

That evening, I watched the pageant of the sunset from the veranda of the bungalow. Directly below me, the evening light had turned the green water of the harbour to beaten silver. A single, unremarkable cloud was touched by the last rays of the sun. One by one, the pale streamers which hung beneath it were charged with gold: the heart of the cloud glowed scarlet. I thought again of Justine and Luis together in Madeira and I was overwhelmed by an almost unbearable sadness.

I spent the morning and afternoon of the next day in my bungalow. The muscles of my calves ached sullenly, and there were broken blisters on both heels. I sat on the veranda, shaded from the sun by the coconut thatch above my head, looking out with unfocussed eyes towards the horizon. Somewhere out beyond that fine blue thread, the men of Angelina were fishing the waters of the banks – absorbed only in the task at hand with no time or inclination for self-indulgent thought.

Sensing my mood, perhaps, Apparani came and went in silence on bare feet. I ate without appetite. Afterwards, I took up my sketch pad again to attempt the long view of the valley behind my house. A sudden gust of wind lifted the paper as I was applying my crayon. I moved to hold the paper on the board and the crayon itself slipped from my fingers and was lost in the grass beside the easel. I tried again; but I could find no pleasure or fulfilment in the task.

Another gust of wind, fragrant with the scent of cinnamon and more powerful than the rest, tore the sheet of paper from the easel. It was lifted into the air like a kite, invested with a brief, mad life of its own, and then deposited in the branches of the star apple tree beyond the kitchen.

I folded the easel and made my way into the bungalow to ask Apparani to point out the way to O'Malloran's house.

CHAPTER VII

O'Malloran's house clung insecurely to a spur of the hill which overlooked the village. It was propped up at the front by three misshapen hardwood pillars, which gave it a curious, predatory aspect. There had been no attempt to maintain the garden which had once surrounded it. A tangle of purple lake bougainvillea had been allowed to run wild and, with time, the long, arched stems of the vines had formed an unintended screen about three sides of the bungalow, deflecting the merciful on-shore breeze at night. The coconut thatch, which had once roofed the front veranda, was rotten with neglect: long tendrils of decay hung down towards the packed earth floor. There were no chairs on the veranda, only a pair of wooden stools with a tea crate set between them to serve as a table. The top of the crate had been covered with a sheet of plastic decorated with an incongruous pattern of grinning clowns.

O'Malloran had returned from his evening labour on the wall only a few minutes before my arrival. He was lighting a hurricane lantern in his kitchen and he came out with the lantern in his hand when he heard my footsteps on the gravel path. The yellow light, shining upwards, accentuated the dark shadows beneath his eyes. He had been at work in the clinic until late the previous night and again all morning. He looked tired, irascible and surprisingly frail.

He scarcely troubled to return my greeting. He said only: 'You better come in and sit down while I get us something to eat. If you need a drink, there's a bottle of rum on the table inside and you should find a glass in the cupboard by the door. I will leave the lantern with you.'

I offered to help him with the meal. He shook his head.

'That,' he said pointedly, 'is something I can manage on my own.'

I sat alone in what evidently served as O'Malloran's living room. The wick of the hurricane lantern had not been trimmed: a thin column of blue-black smoke rose from one corner of the flame and stained the inside of the glass mantle. I fumbled for the serrated metal knob and turned down the flame. The column of smoke vanished abruptly, but the light of the lantern was reduced now to little more than a feeble orange glow.

From the direction of the kitchen, I could hear the intermittent rattle of saucepans and the sound of my host blowing into the base of his coalpot to stimulate the fire he had set among the sticks of charcoal. I decided that a smoking lantern was better than one which gave no light. I turned up the wick again to look about me.

The planks of the uncarpeted floor were caked with sand and soil brought in on O'Malloran's worn out tennis shoes. In the centre of the room there was a table with one missing leg. A wooden keg with rusting metal hoops had been provided to serve in place of the absent leg. The keg was an inch too short, and the bottle of rum which stood on the table was in imminent danger of sliding to the floor. A fragment of patterned linen had been draped over the table, but the exact nature of the pattern had been obscured long ago by a series of dun coloured stains and festering orange peel. Three metal chairs were drawn up to the table: a fourth chair, the one on which I was sitting, had been set down near the doorway. Apart from the cupboard which occupied the opposite corner – and in which O'Malloran had said there was a glass – the room was bare of furniture.

The whitewashed walls of the room were streaked with water stains. There were no pictures on the walls – only a cheap coloured map of the Caribbean. A thick red circle had been drawn around the fleck of green which represented Angelina in the top half of the map. There was no trace anywhere of a book or a magazine. I took up the lantern from the table and opened the cupboard door. Inside, there were two enamel mugs and a glass tumbler. The tumbler had not been washed since it was last used: a thin grey sediment had dried hard about the rim. A pair of cockroaches fled at the unexpected access of light. I could hear the dry rustle of their wing cases as they scrambled for refuge in the shadows at the back of the cupboard. I closed the door with the side of my shoe.

O'Malloran returned from the kitchen. He was carrying a loaf of bread and two enamel bowls filled with what smelt like fish stew. He put the bowls on the table and broke the bread in half with his coarse, scarred hands. He motioned to me to sit down. We began to eat by the light of the smoking lantern. A straw coloured moth blundered into the glass mantle and fell crippled on the table beside my meal.

The evening breeze had died away early that night, and the untamed hedge around the house sealed in the heat which it had trapped during the course of the long afternoon. There were chillies in O'Malloran's stew. I mopped my face with one of the large white handkerchiefs which had been Justine's last birthday present to me. O'Malloran did not seem to feel the heat.

When we had finished, he said: 'We better sit outside. I want to talk to you.'

I followed him on to the veranda of the house. We sat on the wooden stools beneath the decaying thatch of the roof. I braced my back against the wall of the building in a futile attempt to make myself more comfortable. The pitted surface of the limestone blocks was hard against my spine. I could feel the stone giving up the stored heat of the afternoon sun. Through a narrow interval in the surrounding wall of bougainvillea, I could just make out the shape of the village below us. There were few lights anywhere: the fishermen and their families were already asleep.

O'Malloran reached into the pocket of his trousers and fetched out a stained clay pipe. He filled it slowly with awkward fingers and stretched his legs out in front of him. He did not appear to notice the discomfort of his backless seat. He drew deeply on his pipe. I shifted my position on my own wooden seat. The stench of uncured tobacco was heavy on the still air. There was movement in the thatch above my head as some small creature crept away from the rising pillar of smoke. I waited.

'I want you to know something about the people of this island,' O'Malloran said at last without preamble, inspecting the bowl of his pipe. 'Perhaps if you understand it will make a difference to how long you remain here.'

I said nothing.

He made a clumsy, unexpected movement with his arms as if to embrace the whole island and its people in that one awkward, sweeping gesture. The harshness of his voice fell away for the first time as he spoke of them.

'You must understand,' he said, 'they are not like other West Indians. Their race was living here and on Manzanilla for a thousand years before the conquistadores came this way. The Spanish exterminated them on Manzanilla. Only here on Angelina were they left in peace. Even Cortes could see there was no gold here.'

His pipe went out: he leant forward and emptied the bowl on the earthen floor at his feet.

'I am talking about a simple people,' he said. 'They do not see the world as we do. In their own language, they have no word for envy or for malice. They do not understand that other people are not like them. They have no defences against the rest of us.'

He spread his arms wide again in that curious, awkward gesture. There was something messianic about his zeal. There are less than four hundred of them left now,' he said hoarsely. They are the last of their kind, and they should be doubly precious because they are a reminder of what the rest of us might be.'

I looked out into the darkness: the moon had passed behind a cloud. O'Malloran filled his pipe again and lit a match. The flame sputtered and died.

'What do they call themselves?' I asked.

'Kakwacha, ' O'Malloran said. 'It means children of the sea.'

I knew the name; it evoked for me at once another clear memory of my childhood. It was afternoon at Sans Souci, the day before my ninth birthday. I had wandered down to the stream which flowed through the tall bamboo. There, in the soft red mud at the edge of the water, I had seen something unfamiliar thrown up by a land crab excavating a fresh hole earlier in the day. It was an object the size of my palm and I was sure that it was not a stone. I bent down, drew it out of the mud and held it in the flowing water to wash it clean. Slowly, almost imperceptibly, the layers of mud dissolved to disclose a terracotta face: the sensitive, finely modelled features gazed up at me from beneath the surface of the water. Flushed with excitement, I had carried my prize back to the house where my parents had examined it dutifully but without interest.

Later that same week, a neighbouring planter had come to tea with my parents. I had left the terracotta image on the veranda table around which they sat. Our guest noticed it as he reached for an ashtray. He picked it up and turned it over in his hands.

'Where did this come from?' he asked my father.

Old Hannah was despatched to fetch me from the

beach so that I could tell again of my discovery. Then all four of us had walked down to the stream within the bamboo grove. Before darkness fell that evening, we had dug out of the undercut bank fragments of six decorated cooking pots and a pair of granite axe heads.

Unlike my parents, our neighbour knew all about them. 'These were made by the Kakwacha,' he said. 'They were the people the Spanish found when they arrived here. They put them to work clearing the land for sugar cane; then they just died out. They couldn't cope with measles and diseases like that.'

He turned to my father. 'There must have been a Kakwacha settlement beside your stream. They always lived by running water. I've found a few axe heads and other things on my own land. I'm making a collection of them.'

He lit a cigarette. 'I'm sorry the Spanish didn't take more care of them,' he said. 'They say they were an amiable lot. They welcomed the conquistadores as brothers when they first arrived. If they had survived, we would never have had to bring the blacks here from Africa...'

As our neighbour rose to leave, I heard my father say casually: 'If you want any of those bits and pieces to swell your collection then take them with you. I hope the owners had better luck with their crops than I'm having with mine this year...'

Later that night in my bedroom, I remember weeping silent tears into my pillow. I had wanted to keep those Indian relics for myself – and the neighbour had taken not only what we had found together in the mud that afternoon, but also the smiling terracotta head which I had discovered entirely on my own.

Next morning, I had risen at first light and fetched a spade from the stable down to the bank of the stream. But although I worked until my mother summoned me for breakfast, and again in the afternoon, I could find no other traces of the people who had lived on our land all those years ago. For the rest of my years at Sans Souci, I was conscious of a presence in the shade of the bamboo grove beside the stream which I had not sensed before. The presence was benign and comforting and, though I really knew that it existed only in my mind, I had always felt a curious empathy with the shades of the people who had preceded me in that quiet place.

'I want you to help me with the wall,' O'Malloran said again. 'If you work in the boat and pass me the rocks, I can finish the job in half the time. After that, you can go on your way.'

I had given thought to the wall earlier in the day. The whole enterprise was laughable. The first storm-driven waves to roll in through the constricted neck of the bay would scatter the loosely packed rocks all over the sea floor. Any captive turtles would swim straight out to the deep water. It was obvious that O'Malloran had taken no account of the hurricane season. At the same time, it was equally apparent that nothing I might say would deflect him from his purpose.

I said: 'Why don't you ask some of the local men to lend you a hand?' thinking that their opinion of the project would be enough to convince him that he was wasting his time.

I could see him glaring at me in the moonlight. 'They have many other things to do. I will not use their help,' he said stubbornly. 'I want to do this thing for them myself. It must be my own gift for Angelina.'

'You run the clinic for them,' I said. 'Isn't that enough?'

O'Malloran was silent for a long moment. I thought mistakenly that he was giving weight to what I had said. An owl called from the darkness beyond the screen of bougainvillea.

So softly that I almost missed the words, I heard him say at last: 'It can never be enough.'

I waited for him to say more but be was silent. We sat uncomfortably together under the rotting thatch. O'Malloran fiddled with his pipe; I listened to the sounds of the night. Eventually I looked at my watch. The luminous hands showed I had scarcely been there an hour.

'You had better go now,' O'Malloran said. 'I need to prepare the clinic for tomorrow morning.'

He turned to look at me in the pale light.

'If you change your mind about helping on the wall you will know where to find me.' He pressed the backs of his hands to his eyes like a thwarted child. 'I couldn't get Brucknor to help either,' he said.

I climbed off my stool, said goodnight and began to walk back the way I had come. I was stiff and still hungry. I half wished that I had said to the importunate man: 'Look, the fact is I haven't space for other people's burdens. I carry quite enough of my own…'; but I knew my own troubles would be nothing to him.

At the summit of the hill, the moon broke cover and lit up the thatched roof of my house. A potoo called from somewhere beneath the guango tree. When I was a child that wild nocturnal cry beyond my bedroom window would conjure up all kinds of threatening images. I looked now at the three quarter moon and thought that here on Angelina, that same evocative call seemed to harbour no trace of threat or malice.

CHAPTER VIII

As I waited for a vessel to return me to Manzanilla, I toyed again with my pastels and sketch pad. Long ago, in the first months after I had given up at art school, I had sometimes wondered whether I might have been too hasty – whether granted a little more time, a certain talent might have emerged after all. Now, the discarded sheets of paper which gathered around the legs of the easel convinced me beyond any doubt that my judgement had been sound. Journalism, it seemed, was the only talent I possessed.

Each afternoon, I walked down from my bungalow to the sea – choosing to avoid the bay where O'Malloran laboured on his futile wall. I had borrowed a face mask from the cacique's shop and, with its help, I renewed an old acquaintance with the reef fish and the molluscs of the inshore water. In one shallow, sandy depression in the middle of an eel grass bed, I came upon the empty shell of a fallow deer cowry. I picked up the shell and held it in the palm of my hand, caressing the polished surface with my fingertips. After a long moment's hesitation, I left it there upon the sand where it belonged.

On the morning of my seventh day on the island, Horst Brucknor sent his man-servant to my house with an invitation to dinner that evening. 'Come as you are,' Brucknor wrote. 'We do not stand on ceremony in this place.' And as a postscript, he added thoughtfully: 'If you would like Auguste to show you the way when the time comes, please so instruct him.'

With some difficulty, I got Auguste to understand that I would find my own way there, since Brucknor had pointed out the path when he had come to call. The Haitian nodded and left as silently as he had arrived.

I set out for Brucknor's house just before the evening light began to fail. Although the place was less than a mile away, the walk took time. The narrow path Brucknor had shown me clung tightly to the hillside before it dropped away to the valley floor and led from there to the sea. Everywhere about me, stands of estrelitzia and scarlet heliconia sprang from the over-hanging bank and narrowed the track. A shallow, chattering stream ran down the centre of the valley with the path beside it.

Brucknor's little house overlooked the sea not far from the spot where the track met the broader coastal path I had followed round the island two days earlier. I could remember looking up the track as I passed by that afternoon and wondering exactly where it led. Immediately in front of the clapboard building, a rough red cedar plank had been raised up on two squat coral pillars to serve as a table. There was an empty cigarette packet on the table and one of those old fashioned silver plated lighters, the plating worn down to the base metal on either side. An empty glass stood on the ground beside one of the wooden chairs.

Brucknor was waiting for me on the steps of his house.

'I saw you approaching,' he said in greeting. 'You did not require Auguste.'

In spite of his note to 'come as you are', he himself had put on a pale blue linen suit. A triangle of faded scarlet handkerchief showed in the breast pocket of the jacket and I saw that both sleeves had been patched more than once at the elbow. He bowed slightly from the waist as we shook hands. I was conscious again of the discreet smell of bay rum – and the dated manners of another place.

'It is good of you to come, Mr Fielding,' he said formally. 'I do not have many guests and you are especially welcome.'

He led the way inside.

The bungalow consisted of a living room – lit now by a cluster of brass kerosene lamps – a single cramped bedroom and a narrow veranda which ran the full length of three sides. There was an outside kitchen and a lean-to attached to it for Auguste to sleep in – and that was all.

The living room was furnished with a wicker-work sofa, a round wooden table and three wicker chairs. An antique spring driven gramophone stood on what had once been a fashionable drinks cabinet. The door of the cabinet had been removed and the shelves inside were stacked with records of the same vintage as the gramophone itself. But it was the glass-fronted mahogany bookcases, standing incongruously against all four walls, which transformed the simple room.

The bookcases were beautifully made, their glass panes bevelled at the edges and each door fitted with an old fashioned brass lock and key. They reached from the floor to the open ceiling. The books they protected were bound in pale, matching calfskin, the titles all embossed in gold. At the base of their spines, each book carried a reference number written in ink on a small square of cream paper; the collection was catalogued just as in a public library before the introduction of computers. Most of the titles, I noticed, were in German, and I remember thinking as I looked around me that the unprepossessing little bungalow was entirely redeemed by the unexpected treasure it contained.

The only picture in the room – in fact there was no space for more than one – hung above the doorless entrance to Brucknor's bedroom. It was a delicate pencil sketch of the Schlossberg at Graz. Justine and I had visited the place on an Austrian holiday not long after we were married and I remembered it well.

Brucknor gestured towards the books. 'They are my life's extravagance,' he said. 'I have had all my life this love of fine books, and even now I am not sure whether it is a blessing or a curse.'

From the direction of the outside kitchen there was a sudden clatter of saucepans. Brucknor stood up. 'If you will excuse me,' he said lightly, 'I will see what Auguste may be doing to our meal.'

In his absence I made another inspection of the bookcases. In the shadowy interval between two cabinets, I noticed a curtained space. Thinking that the curtain concealed more books, I leant forward and drew it aside. Pinned taut to a plywood frame against the wall hung an oil-stained naval ensign. On the wall beneath it was a row of seven or eight black and white photographs. I looked closely: all but one I saw, were unremarkable pictures of submarines at sea or of little groups of naval officers, their service caps worn rakishly over one eye. The picture at the extreme end of the row, however, was more formal. It was of a very young Korvetten-capitan being invested with his Knight's Cross by a familiar figure wearing a service cap of his own and a brown raincoat. The man in the raincoat was saying something to the young hero, whose face was lit up with pride at the honour being paid him. In the space at the bottom of the photograph, Brucknor had written simply: *Kiel. 23 Juni 1943.*

With a curious feeling of guilt at having intruded where I was not meant to go, I pulled the curtain shut and resumed my inspection of the books. Brucknor returned a moment later. Seeing my interest, he took a key from a small bunch at his waist and opened one of the glazed doors. He reached up and selected a pair of books from their place on the shelves. He stroked their supple bindings, caressing the pale leather with a lover's touch.

'Sometimes I feel that I would have done better to

have paid more attention to their contents,' he said, 'but I love each of them just for what they are. Perhaps they are the children I never had...'

The meal was served by Auguste, dressed now in a white jacket darned twice at the collar and missing two of its flat brass buttons at the cuff. The main course was baked red snapper into which Brucknor had inserted little strips of lobster and pimento spice. The fish lay in a shallow bath of a thick sauce flavoured with coconut milk. He dismissed my compliments with a modest wave of his hand. 'I am more skilled with European fish,' he said. 'The flavour is less coarse...'

Afterwards, we sat together on two of the wicker chairs which Auguste moved onto the back veranda of the house, overlooking the sea. Silent and unsmiling, Auguste brought us coffee and two tumblers of cognac. A three quarter moon lit up the crescent beach. The familiar fragrance of white jasmine was heavy on the night air. I leant back in my chair and thought of O'Malloran and the very different life he led on the little island. After a while, I decided to ask Brucknor to tell me something more about the man. It must be good, I suggested, to have the company of another European on Angelina. He did not agree.

'I am sorry to say the man does not care for me,' he said. 'At heart he is an ascetic – and ascetics make uncomfortable companions. The people of the island love him; they would look after him better if they could, but he will not allow it. He is one of those who would wear a hair shirt every day if he could find one. He neglects himself and cares only for them. He is an unhappy man and there is no cure for it.'

He cradled his tumbler in the palms of both hands.

'At the beginning, we got on well enough. I used to watch him at work in his clinic. He had once trained as a doctor, but then he had entered the Church and for many years he had served as a priest. Once – while we were still friends – he told me how he had come to lose his faith. Later, he explained his plan to breed turtles on Angelina. He asked me to help him raise a sea wall to enclose the bay. I told him I was too old for that kind of work. Since then, he has not sought my company.' He swallowed a mouthful of cognac. 'In any case, it was always clear that the idea was ridiculous. That kind of unsupported structure will never hold.'

Brucknor got up and walked over to his gramophone. He knelt down, chose a record from the cabinet beneath it and wound up the clockwork machine. There was the prolonged hiss of a steel needle in the groove, and then the prelude to 'Lohengrin' drifted out into the soft Caribbean night. In the brief interval while he turned the record, he said quietly: 'As a boy, I used to travel to Bayreuth every year before the war. The most important people were gathered there for the Festival. It was very beautiful and the music sometimes brings it back to me after all those years. They were exciting times... full of hope for the future of our country and for the righting of the wrongs we had endured...'

Auguste returned with more coffee. Brucknor changed the records. He owned three different versions of 'The Ride of the Valkyries' and we heard each of them twice. After that, there was Bach and Beethoven and a little Mozart. At midnight, I stood up to go.

'It was good of you to come,' Brucknor said formally. 'It is not often now that I have the pleasure of entertaining people whose company I can enjoy. I hope you will come again...'

He insisted that I should carry a hurricane lantern with me on my way home. Auguste was despatched to find and light it. Brucknor walked with me to the point where the track up the valley swung away from the broader coastal path. I said goodnight and, with the uncertain help of the old lantern, found my way back to my bungalow in spite of the steepness of the track and the delayed effects of the brandy.

I did not feel like sleep. I sat on the veranda of the house and looked out at the shifting patterns of moonlight on the dark canopy of the rain forest, and I wondered why a man of Brucknor's taste and interests should have chosen to spend the evening of his life on Angelina where the only other European resident was a man who possessed neither books nor paintings nor the smallest interest in anything but the people he was driven to serve.

CHAPTER IX

Next morning, the cacique's boy arrived with a message as I was finishing breakfast. Apparani showed him into the house.

I thought I knew why he was there. 'Does the schooner come today?' I asked before he could speak.

The boy shook his head. 'My father send me for a different purpose,' he said apologetically. 'He send me to say a mwaitan is called for the village tonight. He wish you will come. It will start seven o'clock in the square.'

I turned to Apparani. 'What is a mwaitan?' I asked. 'What is it all about?'

She searched for words to explain to a stranger what had always been a familiar part of her life. 'It is when we meet together.' she said. 'It is when all of us come to the one place. Then we remember who we are and we talk of anything that troubles us... and we eat together and there is music and we dance.'

I had thought the boy had been sent to tell me that I would be able to leave Angelina. I put aside my disappointment.

'Tell the cacique I will come,' I said.

The boy started down the hill again and Apparani began to clear the table.

'Our people will be glad you are with them,' she said softly.

In the evening, I went to my case to find a clean shirt. As I fumbled among the clothes I had not unpacked, my fingers closed around the frame of the photograph of Justine. I drew it out of the case.

'With all my love forever, darling,' she had written hastily across one corner, over the swell of her breasts.

I arrived at the square beneath the royal palm as the ceremony of the mwaitan was about to begin. The cacique's son had been looking out for me. The boy greeted me gravely and led me to a little group of chairs at the head of the square. The smooth, grey trunk of the palm tree at its centre melted into the darkness of the night above my head. The boy showed me where to sit. In the pale light of the kerosene lanterns I saw that I had been placed next to O'Malloran. The man looked round but made no move to greet me. There were seats, too, for Brucknor and Miss Katy, but neither of them had arrived.

The square was filled with people. They were sitting on plain wooden benches and everyone had dressed for the occasion. Those men who owned jackets had put them on over plaid shirts without collars. The women wore dresses they had fashioned for themselves, the thin cloth decorated in bold, abstract patterns. The dresses of the unmarried women were tight-waisted, with short, stiffened skirts that flared out from the hips. Unlike the men, the women had chosen to remain barefoot. They wore flowers in their hair – pink hibiscus or sprays of white jasmine. The square was full of the fragrance of the jasmine and of the sound of people greeting each other.

Not far from where I sat, I saw Apparani. Beside her on the bench was another girl who could only have been her sister, a baby at her breast and a child playing at her feet.

The cacique was sitting two places to my left. He pushed back his chair and stood up. The people in the square stopped talking and the mothers hushed their children. The cacique began in the old language of his people. He spoke slowly, without hesitation but with occasional, deliberate intervals of silence as though he wished to give his listeners time to reflect for a moment on what he had just said.

After a while, I leant over and touched O'Malloran on the shoulder. The man smelt faintly of saltwater and sweat.

'What is he saying?' I asked.

O'Malloran turned unwillingly towards me. 'He is recounting the story of his people,' he said gruffly. 'He is reminding them of who they are... of their cousins who were lost on Manzanilla... of their duty to each other... of their love for their island. It is part of the tradition of the mwaitan.'

The cacique brought his address to a close. There was no applause of the usual sort. Instead, there was a kind of deep-throated murmur of approval which started with the man on my right and was taken up in turn by the people all around the square. I turned again to O'Malloran.

'What is the purpose of it all?' I asked.

'It is like I told you,' he said impatiently. 'He was reminding them of their history and of their traditions and of the standards they must live by.' Once again, he rubbed the corners of his eyes with his knuckles like a weary child. 'It is a kind of family ritual: at each mwaitan, the cacique recounts the story of the race. He must use the same form of words each time. It serves to renew the bonds that hold them together.'

I said: 'I thought he was reciting a prayer.'

'It is a prayer of a kind,' O'Malloran said. 'It is a prayer of thankfulness and a promise to hold to the old ways. Their caciques have used the same words in this place for four hundred years.'

I sat back in my chair and looked around me at the family which had come together to remember who they were.

The cacique gave a signal and the second phase of the mwaitan began. A man stood in front of the cacique and addressed the meeting. He was questioned and he gave answers. A general discussion seemed to follow and other men and women rose to their feet and spoke. I remembered that Apparani had told me that one of the purposes of the mwaitan was to allow people to state their grievances.

One of the speakers produced a bamboo float as he spoke. I gathered there was a disagreement about ownership of the fish trap the float had once marked. Another man stepped forward and showed the cacique three shallow notches carved in the wood at one blunt end. The man who had spoken first reached over to examine the marks and then seemed to withdraw his claim. The cacique said a few words and it was clear that the matter was at an end.

The meeting passed on to other matters which I did not understand. Several women spoke. Pra Latana was mentioned by name. People laughed and pointed at him affectionately. O'Malloran laughed with them and I suddenly realised that I had not seen the man smile before. A woman with her child in her arms came out of the seated crowd, kissed his hand and said something to the meeting. I waited until she had resumed her seat and then asked O'Malloran what she had said. This time he just shook his head and did not reply.

After a while, the discussion came to an end and the cacique rose to his feet again.

'I speak in English now, ' he said, 'because we have with us here a guest who does not yet know our language.' He turned and put his large hand lightly on my shoulder. 'We do not see many visitors on Angelina and we hope his stay with us will be contented.'

He paused for a moment: a light breeze played in the leaves of the ancient palm tree high above our heads.

'Since the last time we met in this place,' the cacique said, 'these of our people have left us behind.' He recited slowly the names of five men and women and the settlements to which they had belonged. 'We remember them with lightness in our hearts and with the knowledge of our ancestors that death cannot separate the Kakwach from each other or from this island which holds them now in its embrace for ever.'

There was a long moment of silence in the square. A baby cried and was comforted. The cacique spoke again.

'Now we greet the new members of our family,' he said.

There was movement among the people on the benches and, one by one, the mothers of Angelinos born since the last gathering rose to present their children to the mwaitan. The cacique locked his large hands together and held them briefly over each child's head in turn. Apparani's sister's child was the last to be introduced. The baby was asleep in her mother's arms and did not wake as she was held up so that everyone could see.

That same curious deep-throated murmur of approval which had followed the cacique's address now filled the square again. It swelled briefly and then died away. There had been five deaths and seven births and the people were content.

The cacique turned towards me. 'Now it is time for us to eat,' he said, 'and we will serve our guest first as is our custom.'

He led me to a long table at the back of the square. The table was covered with a sheet of bleached coconut matting on which the meal had been laid out. I took up a wooden spoon and helped myself to strips of kingfish and baked lambi. I filled my plate with sea urchin roe, with yam and sweet potato baked in their jackets, and with pale slices of boiled christophine. The cacique poured me a glass of white rum, added a measure of sweetened lime juice and grated a nutmeg over the surface of the drink.

The moon had risen while the mwaitan was in progress. From where I sat I could look down the length of the sandy street to the head of the wooden jetty where I had first stepped ashore. A broad band of moonlight was laid across the harbour water, and moonlight filled the square and rested softly on the people of the island and their children.

When everyone had eaten, the cacique called out to an old man sitting at the base of the palm tree in the centre of the square.

'What does he want the old man to do?' I asked O'Malloran.

'You will have noticed we have no television here,' O'Malloran said sardonically. 'We rely on an older form of entertainment. The old man is the mwaitanatan – the story teller.'

The mwaitanatan was a spare old man with thick white hair and a seamed fisherman's face. He did not look at his audience as he got to his feet. His eyes seemed to be focussed on some far distant point beyond the moonlit mouth of the harbour. Then, as he was led to a high stool beside the cacique, I realised that he was blind.

He climbed on to the stool. There was a long moment of silence – the silence of expectation. Then the old man began his stories.

From the beginning, it scarcely seemed to matter that I could not understand the words he used. The tone of his voice – leaping from one octave to another – and the movement of his hands, stabbing and chopping the air in front of him, spoke their own universal language.

He began with stories that everyone had clearly heard before – the same stories, I thought, that had probably been told by the mwaitanatans of the island for longer than anyone present could remember. At the climax of each story, the audience would chant the final lines in company with the old man and the square would be rocked with shouts of laughter at the old, familiar jokes. Then, abruptly, the old man would change the mood: there would be a story that evidently touched some deep chord of sadness, instantly reflected in the dark faces of the people who listened spellbound on the benches in front of him.

For more than an hour, there was no sound in the square beneath the canopy of the palm tree except the old man's voice, the laughter and despair of his audience, and the occasional cry of a waking baby in its mother's arms. Then, without warning or flourish, the story teller came to the end of his repertoire. The cacique got to his feet and led the old man reverently back to his place among the people. Once again, that curious, deep-throated murmur of approval filled the square. The mwaitanatan lifted his hand in brief acknowledgement and slipped back into the shadows.

Released from the spell of his art, people came to life again. They left their seats and began to walk around the square for the first time that evening, greeting friends and relatives from the outer settlements. People came up to greet O'Malloran and to inquire about his health.

One woman took his large hands in hers, examined the wounds inflicted by the limestone rocks and said something I did not understand. O'Malloran withdrew his hands and pressed them lightly against the woman's cheeks. The woman returned to her family in the crowd and I asked O'Malloran who she was. He reached into his pocket for his clay pipe.

'She lost her husband last month,' he said. 'He was injured and he died in the clinic. If I had had the equipment, I could have saved him.'

A space was cleared in one corner of the square and a little group of musicians took their places. I saw that there was a man with an ancient fiddle, another with a set of pan-pipes and two more with a goat-skin drum and an iron triangle. The wooden benches were pushed back to the edge of the square and, at a signal from the cacique, the orchestra began to play.

At first, the rhythms were slow and restrained. The men and women who came into the middle to dance were mostly of my own generation. The younger ones looked on patiently and chattered among themselves and, after a while, almost imperceptibly, the pace of the music quickened and the beat of the drum became more pronounced. More and more people entered the dance beneath the canopy of the royal palm.

I caught sight of Apparani. She was playing with her sister's child. The light of the lanterns glistened on her loose, dark hair. The cacique appeared at my side.

'You should dance with her,' he said.

I shook my head. 'I am just looking on,' I heard myself say stiffly. 'I am not part of this.'

'I think perhaps we are all part of this,' the cacique said, and joined the dancers himself.

The dancers overflowed among the benches and spilled out beyond the circle formed by the flickering lanterns. Every child who could walk became part of the dance, leaping and spinning to the beat of the music with that sure and perfect sense of rhythm which I soon learnt was the birthright of every Angelino.

In spite of myself, the insistent beat of the music took hold of me as well. I found myself moving purposefully through the press of heaving bodies towards the place where I had last seen Apparani. The girl was still beside her sister. She was dressed in a simple white frock gathered lightly at the waist by a belt of coconut fibre. Like all the other women, her legs were bare and she wore no shoes.

As I approached, the music ceased. I hesitated awkwardly, but it was only a brief hiatus to allow the fiddler to tighten his bow string. By the time I reached the girl, the musicians had launched into a slower, more sedate piece of music of their own composition. The man with the pan-pipes began to sing and his voice drowned my own words. I pointed first to myself and then towards the swaying mass of people behind me in the square. The girl came to me without a word. I noticed that a number of lanterns at the edge of the square had now gone out. I guided us both to a space between two benches. We collided briefly with another couple: for a moment I felt the softness of the girl's dark hair against my face. We danced on, around the outer edge of the crowd.

I stumbled and nearly lost my balance. The girl looked up at me and laughed. Then the drummer made a final, premature flourish, the music came untidily to an end and someone brought a tray of drinks to the musicians.

I returned Apparani to her sister. The baby looked at me with huge dark eyes. I made my way out of the square and walked down the sandy street towards the jetty and the quiet water of the deserted harbour. Somewhere, just inside the passage through the coral, a school of needle gars leapt clear of the water in a cascade of phosphorescence. I sat down on the bollard to which my schooner had tied up.

My thoughts were unfocussed: I tried for a moment to imagine that I was back in London. I was describing to Justine the course of the past two weeks, but I could see that none of it held any interest for her. She did not like small islands. Once, early in our marriage, I had taken her to the Isles of Scilly. I had planned that we should stay two weeks. By the end of the second day, Justine had wanted to move on.

'I can't help it, darling,' she had said. 'Places like this make me feel uncomfortable. I need people around me and buildings and proper streets and things like that. Yesterday, we were the only people on the whole of that long beach.'

We had returned to London the following day and on our next holiday I had taken her to Paris. We stayed in a hotel on the Rue de Rivoli where she had seemed content.

I did not return to the dance. Some time after

midnight I walked home. The coral surface of the road glowed white in the moonlight. Below me, from the dimly lit village square, the music of the fiddle and the pipes rose into the night air like smoke from a cedarwood fire. The people were singing now the old songs of their race, the women alone at first and then the men and then all of them in harmony.

I stopped for breath halfway up the hill and thought of O'Malloran and what he had told me: 'They are a special people… they are uncorrupted by the rest of us… they should be doubly precious, because they are a reminder of what the rest of us might be.'

For the first time, I felt that I could understand something of what it was that drove the man to cherish and protect them with that single-minded, obsessive zeal which took no account of obstacles in its path and admitted no opinion but his own.

CHAPTER X

Next morning, I met Miss Katy.

With nothing to do while I waited for the arrival of the schooner, I walked down to the village with the unformed idea of offering to help O'Malloran in some way with the work at his clinic. As I turned into the main street, I saw a tall, elegant white woman standing in the shade at the entrance to the cacique's shop. She was talking to the cacique himself who had come out of his shop to greet her.

She caught sight of me, said something to the cacique, touched him affectionately on the arm and crossed over the dirt road. She wore a pair of cotton slacks and a faded pale blue blouse, the colour of her eyes.

'I have not been hospitable,' she said at once in greeting. 'You must let me put that right...'

Five minutes later I had agreed to visit her the following afternoon.

'Come for tea,' she said. 'I can't offer you cucumber sandwiches, but I can promise salmagundi and casava biscuits baked in my own kitchen.'

We talked for a while there at the side of the road

and then I watched as she walked back through the little village in the direction of her own house overlooking the sea. As she passed by, I saw that the women came out of their houses with their children to wave to her. She seemed to have a word for them all and some of the smaller children ran up to hold her hand for a moment and to tell her they were glad to see her there.

At the clinic, I found that O'Malloran had left to visit a patient in one of the little settlements beyond the village. I abandoned the idea of helping him and, after a circuit of the village and an exchange of greetings with the cacique who had remained outside his shop, I climbed the hill again and returned to my house.

I arrived at Miss Katy's place promptly at half past three the next afternoon. The look of the sprawling house with its shingled roof was at once familiar to me: it was a scaled down version of the kind of well proportioned, jalousie-windowed, high-ceilinged estate house that every wealthy planter had sooner or later built for his family in the old days on Manzanilla. This one, as she told me later, had been built on Angelina by her grandfather, and it had served as the family's holiday retreat, which they visited faithfully twice a year when she had been a child.

Miss Katy was waiting for me on the veranda at the back of the house above the beach. We sat in old-fashioned, upholstered wicker chairs with a round, wicker table set down between us. A girl in a white maid's apron brought out tea and casava biscuits, still warm from the oven. Almost at once, our conversation turned to Manzanilla and what had become of the planter families we had both known. I asked about her own family's estate. I remembered it well: we used to pass its high wrought iron gates on our monthly journeys from our own small property on the coast to the capital town on the opposite side of the island. Through the open ironwork, you could see – at the head of the long, tree-lined drive – the imposing Great House itself. I could tell that the subject of her estate was painful still to Miss Katy.

'After independence, the government took over our land,' she said. 'Two years later they seized the house. They said they needed it for an agricultural college, but they never used it for that purpose. One of their ministers lives in it now.'

She had moved to Florida with her parents after the loss of the estate. She had married a professor at the university at Orlando but the marriage had not been a success and they had gone their separate ways. There had been no children, and she said this without sadness. Afterwards, she had lived for several years at Fort Lauderdale and then in a house on the beach on Sanibel. She did not say it, but it was clear that there had been other men in her life after her divorce – though she did not marry again. Eventually, she tired of life in Florida and decided to return to the West Indies to live in the holiday home on Angelina, which had passed to her when her parents died.

I asked how she managed to keep herself occupied on Angelina.

'I write stories,' she said, 'but recently the market for stories set on small Caribbean islands seems to have moved on. They don't appear to want them any more.'

She looked out across the bay to the open sea. 'Sometimes I think I have become a kind of ancient sea creature abandoned on this island by the tide…' And she smiled her charming, self-deprecating smile to show that she didn't really believe the words herself.

Each morning, she said, she still sat down at her desk to write for three hours before lunch, but now it was really more an exercise in mental discipline, and she had given up sending her stories to the literary magazines and the ladies' journals which had once bought them from her and often paid well. I guessed that the failure of this source of income was a more serious matter than she was willing to admit.

She was growing old now, but it was not difficult to see that thirty years ago she had been a beautiful woman. She had kept her figure, though there were deeply etched networks of lines around her eyes and at the corners of her mouth. There was a defiant quality about her, and her voice was the voice of a much younger woman. I quickly realised that she had not yet surrendered to the years and intended to enjoy in every way whatever time still lay ahead of her.

She spoke of her attachment to Angelina. As the cacique told me, she had been born on the island. It had not been planned by her parents – she had arrived without warning four weeks early and there had been no time to take her mother back to their Manzanillan estate for the birth. In the event, the cacique's aunt had served as midwife and the birth was easy.

'I am glad I was born here,' she said looking out over the golden beach. I have always felt a special bond with Angelina and its people...'

She talked about her childhood memories of the island and – unlike Manzanilla and the other islands of the Caribbean – how little had changed over the years. 'But we need to be realistic,' she said softly. 'No society these days can remain fixed in amber.'

It was dark by the time I left and I knew there would be no moon until much later in the night. I returned to my bungalow on the hill by way of the village and the serpentine road with its pale coral surface, which seemed to emit a dull light of its own even when the moon was down.

CHAPTER XI

At the beginning of my third week on Angelina, when there was still no news of the next schooner to call, I decided – if I could – to bring together Brucknor and O'Malloran. I was curious to see the two men in each other's company; perhaps even to repair the breech between them. I invited them for an evening meal and discussed with Apparani what we ought to provide for them to eat.

Brucknor accepted my invitation politely, without troubling to conceal a sardonic smile. 'I do not think he will come,' he said; but I was not discouraged.

I tracked down O'Malloran to his clinic. It was early afternoon and the man had not yet left to work on his wall. He did not look up as I entered the building: he merely gestured towards a chair in the corner. I sat down. For the next five minutes I watched as he removed a fish hook from the face of a small boy. The hook was embedded deep in the flesh beside the boy's right eye. His mother sat quietly on a stool at his shoulder.

O'Malloran took up a pair of pliers and cut through

the top of the metal shank. Then he drew the hook out cleanly with a single, practised movement of his wrist. For such a large, ungainly man his touch was surprisingly sure and gentle. He swabbed the wound with iodine, but the boy did not flinch.

'Keep it clean,' he said to the boy in English. 'Next time, use your hook on a fish – not on your head.'

The boy nodded solemnly.

'Is it hurting?' O'Malloran asked.

The boy shook his head. 'I do not feel it,' he said.

'Your father would have been proud of you,' O'Malloran said. 'Now take you mother home.'

Through a curtain of threaded jumbie beads I could see into the other room of the little clinic. There was just enough space to accommodate three cots and two of them were occupied. Both patients were asleep. O'Malloran left his desk and went through the bead curtain. One of the patients had vomited in her sleep. O'Malloran fetched a bowl of water and a cloth and began to clean up the mess. I heard the young woman groan in her sleep. When he was finished, he returned to his desk.

'What is wrong with the woman?' I inquired.

'Her skull is fractured,' he said.

'Will she recover?'

'No,' he said. 'She is dying. This clinic does not have what I need to save her.'

He walked over to the basin in the corner of the room, filled it with water from a clay jug and scrubbed his hands.

I said: 'I came to ask you to have a meal with me tomorrow evening.'

'I do not eat out,' he said bluntly.

'I came to your place.'

'I asked you for a purpose,' O'Malloran said.

The woman with the fractured skull woke up at that moment and called out in pain. O'Malloran passed through the bead curtain again to attend to her. He said something softly in her own language and held a mug for her to drink. He came back to his desk after a while and wrote briefly in a file. Then he relented.

'I will come tomorrow,' he said, looking up suddenly from his desk. 'Now I must get on.'

I walked out into the moist heat of the afternoon. There had been a brief shower of rain while I was in the clinic and the coral surface of the roadway steamed in the sun.

Apparani spent the next afternoon preparing the meal. I bought two bottles of rum from the cacique's shop, a paper bag full of limes and a single nutmeg. During the day, I prepared a clay jug of rum punch: it lacked only ice.

In an attempt to improve the look of the table at which we would eat, I put away the hurricane lantern and replaced it with two rough candles which I had found in the table drawer. As darkness fell, I lit the candles, poured myself a drink and waited for my guests.

Brucknor arrived promptly at seven o'clock. O'Malloran, who came directly from his clinic was thirty minutes late. It was clear as soon as he walked into the house that he had not expected to see Brucknor there – and equally clear that he intended to make no attempt to put aside his dislike of the man for the sake of politeness.

We sat down to eat. Ignoring O'Malloran's silent disdain, Brucknor gamely steered the conversation towards subjects that the man might wish to talk about. O'Malloran remained silent.

I asked about the woman lying in his clinic with a fractured skull.

'She is dead,' he said brusquely: that was all.

Brucknor tried again. Were the Kakwacha distantly related to the Maya? he wondered. Geographically speaking, they had lived close to each other before the Spanish came. It was to no purpose. O'Malloran would not be drawn into the conversation. He refused the rum punch I had laboured over and, it seemed to me, ate his meal only because he did not want to hurt Apparani who had prepared it. When she came in to remove his plate, he complimented her in the tone of voice he appeared to reserve only for the Kakwacha themselves. For Brucknor and for me, he could find few words. When the meal was over, he declined coffee, stood up from the table and took his leave.

'I have to be up early,' he said stiffly.

I walked with him to the steps of the bungalow. It had begun to rain and there was no moon to light the way down the hill. He brushed aside my offer of a lantern.

'I am sorry to see you entertaining that man,' was all he said. Then he was gone, his shambling grey figure swallowed up at once in the night.

I returned to the table, regretting now that I had ever thought of persuading O'Malloran to come in the first place. It had been foolish to attempt to reconcile the two men: I had involved myself in something that was none of my business. I should have foreseen the result.

Brucknor was more philosophical. 'You must not concern yourself about his behaviour on my account,' he said without rancour. 'He is an unhappy man. It is a hard thing to lose faith both in your God and in yourself on the same day.'

I asked him what he meant. He leant back in his chair and lit a cigarette.

'He told me about his life one day not long after I arrived here. It was before he had conceived the idea of the wall and we were cordial with each other. Perhaps he thought I could be of use to him. He was a different man then...'

We got up from the table and I led the way on to the veranda where it was cooler. Apparani brought out a fresh jug of coffee and laid it on the wicker table between us. Among the silk cotton trees at the edge of the forest the lamps of the female fireflies went on and off like aerial lighthouses in the darkness. A potoo called once and was answered faintly in the distance.

'It happened about ten years ago,' Brucknor said. 'You may remember it was a time of famine in East Africa: there were pictures of starving children in every newspaper. O'Malloran was a priest somewhere in the west of Ireland. He comes from a family of priests. His congregation saw the pictures one day and decided to adopt a village in the Sudan. They collected money and asked him to go out to the village and relieve the suffering. He flew off to Kampala, hired a Land Rover and a driver and set out to find the village on the other side of the border. It was the dry season and the roads were passable, but he had never in his life seen real suffering before. He had read about it – but that is a different thing. When he arrived, he found a whole people dying. He told me there were children dying on the bare earth beside their mothers... the bodies of children dead outside each hut. The men had left and had not returned, and the dogs were feeding on the bodies of the children, and some of the children were not yet dead when the dogs took them...'

Brucknor looked out into the darkness and lit another cigarette. He expelled the smoke slowly from his lungs.

'He had trained as a doctor for five years before he entered the Church, but that did not help his case. He found that he could not come to terms with what he saw – and what he saw broke his faith. He told me it was a physical thing – he thought he could feel it rupture deep within his body...'

There was a long moment of silence. I began to think that he was not going to tell me any more. His face was hidden from me in the darkness.

'What did he do?' I prompted.

'What he did,' Brucknor said at last, 'explains why he is as he is today. He abandoned the people he had been sent to help. He just left them to their misery and came home with the money still unspent in his case. He had brought along on that first visit a few tins of corned beef and he threw these out on the road in the village and told the driver to take him back. He told me that some of the women who still had the strength spat at him as he left, because they had believed he was going to save them. It is clear that he suffered a nervous collapse.'

Apparani had left the jug of coffee with us. I filled our cups again. An errant firefly settled for a moment on the rim of my cup, illuminating briefly the green band that ran around it.

'He told me everything,' Brucknor said. 'Once he had begun he could not stop. I do not believe he had ever made a full confession to anyone before – I mean with all the details, like the dogs and the children. I do not know why he chose me as the one to tell. Perhaps the burden grew too heavy and there was no one else.'

'How did he end up on Angelina?' I asked.

'He left the Church as soon as he arrived back in Ireland. He told me he worked in a hotel for a while after that, cleaning shoes and carrying suitcases. Then he was left a little money and he tried to settle in America. He drove a taxi in Miami for a year; then he drifted into the Caribbean. I do not know how he came to visit Angelina, but he has been here ever since. As you have seen, he lives now only for the people of this island. He has no life of his own any more.'

'Why does he do it?' I wanted to know.

'It is obvious,' Brucknor said. 'It is because he cannot forgive himself. He failed people who needed him. Now he has found another people who need him. Everything he does for them is his attempt to make up for what happened in Africa. He knows that in his own eyes it will never be enough – but it is all that is left to him.'

He lit another cigarette. The glowing head of the match described a broad arc in the darkness as he flicked it over the veranda rail and on to the gravelled path.

'It is going to rain later tonight,' he said confidently. 'One of the few useful things I have learnt during my stay here is to forecast the weather. I am rarely mistaken.'

I asked how long he had been on Angelina.

'I shall have lived on this rock for exactly twenty-eight months tomorrow,' he said. 'I keep count of the days. I brought with me my books, as you have seen. I also brought Auguste, so I have not been without comforts, but I know now I am not a man made for small islands.'

He looked around him and noticed in the darkness my sketch pad lying where I had left it on the dirt floor.

'You are an artist?' he inquired.

I explained how the pad came to be there. Our conversation turned to painting: it was clear that this was another of his interests. He wanted to tell me about a visit he had made to Port-au-Prince, to 'inspect the Haitian art' as he put it. He had not liked what he saw.

'It is the product of a primitive imagination,' he said. 'There is no technique. It has no merit.'

It was a subject I knew a little about. The year after we were married, I had bought an early Hyppolite for Justine from a gallery off the Charing Cross Road. I had carried the painting back to our flat and hung it in the dining room. But Justine had been of the same opinion as Brucknor. She too had thought it crude. So I had taken it away to the spare bedroom where its brilliant colours had glowed fiercely in the cold English light, and it was admired in secret only by myself. It hung there still.

Brucknor had been watching my expression. 'You do not agree with me,' he said. 'And I am sure it is not a popular view in this part of the world...'

He spoke of the years he had spent in London. It explained his command of the language. He had enjoyed it there; he intended to return in the not too distant future. He liked the people. His one regret was that the city had become swamped by other races: he saw this as a misfortune.

'I know several booksellers there,' he said. 'Occasionally, in the past, they would find a book for me which I liked.'

It was late by the time he stood up to go.

'I am sorry you did not arrive earlier in Angelina,' he said. 'I have missed the stimulus of conversation.'

From the steps of my bungalow, I watched the beam of his torch advance steadily along the side of the mountain; then the path took him into the cover of the trees and the flickering shaft of light faded from sight. A pair of horseshoe bats passed low over the roof of my house, the translucent membranes of their wings silhouetted briefly against the face of the moon.

I lingered a moment on the steps. I wondered what it was that had brought the man to Angelina in the first place. For someone of his tastes those two and a half years must sometimes have been hard to endure.

There was a movement in the shadows behind me and Apparani came from the kitchen to remove the cups from the wicker table. I was sorry that I had not thought to release her long before.

'There was no need to stay so late,' I said.

'It is no matter,' the girl replied quietly. She moved to go, then abruptly turned to face me. To my surprise, I saw that her eyes were full of tears.

So softly that I could scarcely hear the words, she said: 'Pra Latana is a good man. Do not be vexed because sometimes he behaves so. It is only because he wants what is best for us.'

Then, dismayed by her own boldness, she was gone, hurrying off into the night before I could think of a word of comfort.

Later that night, I lay awake on my bed listening to the symphony of the tree frogs somewhere beyond the water tank and to the occasional call of the potoo which went unanswered now. I thought of how O'Malloran had come to lose his faith, and the thought reminded me of the death of my own brief adolescent conviction that there was a God out there who wished us well.

I had been at dinner one evening with my parents when the old cook's granddaughter pulled over on to herself a lighted kerosene lamp. The glass reservoir of the lamp had shattered on the kitchen floor and the burning oil leapt up to embrace her small black body.

I knew the little girl well. In the dusty yard at the back of our house I often picked her up and swung her onto my shoulders. 'Go, Massa race horse,' she used to yell in my ear, digging her bare heels into my ribs, 'gallop like hell.' Then we would charge around the open space, bucking and prancing until horse and rider collapsed together on the kitchen steps.

For more than an hour after the flames had been smothered, the child's cries had echoed through the old wooden house. All down her front to the fork of her legs, the black skin hung in shrivelled folds. She died at last, far too late, as the doctor's car drew up outside.

'If you won't save her,' I remember praying when it was clear she could not live, 'then at least let her die in peace...'

In the weeks that followed, I had sought to find excuses for God's conduct in the affair; not for her death, but for the pointless suffering. It had been no good: the inner space that had briefly contained my faith was filled from then on by an unhappy cynicism which I sought to conceal even from myself.

O'Malloran, I thought enviously, had filled his own bleak emptiness in a very different way.

CHAPTER XII

Four days after my tea with Miss Katy, I was visited again by O'Malloran. I had been out on the reef earlier that afternoon and there was still no word of the schooner's next visit. The muscles of my shoulders ached sullenly. I had poured myself a measure of rum and I intended to turn in as soon as I had finished it. I knew I had spent too long in the water. The rum and my dull fatigue served to bring back a sudden, urgent need for my wife. I got up wearily from my chair as O'Malloran walked into the house.

In the light of the lantern, suspended from a hook above the table, the man looked pale and agitated. I saw that his hands were shaking. He kept them clasped in front of his large body so that I should not see it.

'I need to talk to you,' he said.

I pointed to the chair on the other side of the table and he sat down heavily.

'It is Brucknor,' he said in a voice as unsteady as his hands, and as if the mention of that name alone was enough to explain his presence in my house.

I curbed my irritation and asked: 'What has he done?'

I could see the man struggle to put his thoughts in order before he spoke.

'They are going to build a hotel,' he said at last. 'Brucknor must have sold them his land. There has been talk of a hotel for two or three months now. I believe it explains why he bought his house and the land around it in the first place. He has never wanted to stay for long on this island.'

I didn't understand. 'Do you want a drink?' I asked.

O'Malloran nodded. I fetched another tumbler from the cupboard against the wall and filled it with what was left of the rum.

'The contractors arrive in three days time,' he said. 'Their vessels are already loading at Port Cabrera. They are going to blast a channel in the reef and widen the mouth of the bay where I am building my wall.'

Now I thought I understood. I moved to reassure him.

'Look,' I said as kindly as I could in the circumstances, 'there are other bays on the island just as suitable for your purpose. I saw two or three of them when I walked around the coast. I could show them to you. It doesn't have to be the end of your scheme. You could start again somewhere else.'

From the other side of the table, O'Malloran stared at me with his blood-shot eyes as though he could not believe what he had heard. He brought his glass down hard in front of him; some of the rum flew out of the glass and splashed his salt-stained shirt. His voice was suddenly shrill with exasperation and despair.

'It's not the turtles, for God's sake,' he said. 'Of

course I can build another holding pen. It's not the wall that matters now – it's the hotel.'

He rested both elbows on the table in front of him and rubbed his eyes with the backs of both hands in that exhausted, curiously child-like gesture which had now become familiar to me.

'Are you blind?' he almost shouted. 'Can't you see what a hotel would do to the life of these people? Have you no imagination at all?' He brought his hands together in front of his body again. 'Think of Manzanilla,' he said.

I sat back in my chair. My shoulders ached. Manzanilla. In the silence between us, the image that sprang to mind was that black shroud of asphalt laid over the site of my bamboo grove at Sans Souci, and over the place by the stream where those cousins of Apparani and the cacique had once made their home. I thought of the sterile, shell-less beach beyond it where I had walked with my adolescent heart full of dreams and certainty, under the bright West Indian sky, that life would always be kind to me. Then I recalled the metal fences with their rusting barbed-wire caps, which separated the visitors and the visited like the steel bars of a zoo. And more than any of these things – more vivid and more hurtful – was the memory of the change that had taken place in the nature of the Manzanillan people themselves.

O'Malloran picked up his glass from the table and finished the rum. His coarse, unshaven face was no longer pale: it was flushed now with a furious determination, and I noticed that his hands no longer shook.

'We have to stop the contractors,' he said. 'We must not allow them to start work.' He swung round to face me. 'And you… you must go to see the governor on Grand Trinity. He's got to rule against it.'

I leant forward to adjust the flame of the hurricane lantern which had begun to smoke. I looked across the table at the importunate man.

'Listen,' I said, searching for the words which would excuse me once and for all from any part in what he had in mind, 'I understand how you feel. I wouldn't choose to have a hotel on the island either if anyone asked my own view – but at best you're talking only of delaying the inevitable. Sooner or later, no matter what you do, this little rock pool will be flooded by the tide from the real world outside. You can't keep these people separate from the rest of humanity. The fact is it will happen; and maybe it would be kinder to let it happen now.'

For the second time that evening he looked at me as if I had lost my reason.

'You haven't understood a thing,' he shouted. 'It can be done. We can still preserve the way they live. We can hold back this tide you talk about.'

His hands had begun to shake again and beads of sweat stood out on his forehead. I looked out into the darkness beyond the open doorway. Then – almost against my will – I began to imagine what the little bay would look like with a concrete hotel set down where the grove of coconut palms now stood, and a landing stage built up over the reef beyond the mouth of the bay for the cruise ships to dock alongside. I pictured the village square and the sandy streets that led from it swarming with loud, pink-faced men and women in search of local colour and fulfilment of other kinds under the tropical sun. I could hear the nasal voices and smell the sun tan oil...

I said for the second time: 'I understand how you feel. I wouldn't want to see the island marked in as a cruise ship's port of call either. I like it as it is, but as I told you before, none of this is my business. I will be gone as soon as the next schooner calls, I am not the person you need...'

O'Malloran brought his hands together again in front of his body. He struggled to control his voice.

'There is no one else,' he said flatly. 'There is only you. I will arrange for a boat to Grand Trinity tonight. You must see the governor and explain what is going to happen here. You can get it stopped. This island is still a British territory. You are a British journalist: you have influence. The governor will not listen to me, but he will have to pay attention to you. You can be back here in three days time...'

Apparani came into the room at that moment to clear away the remains of my evening meal. Her eyes lit up with pleasure and surprise to see O'Malloran there. She greeted him in her own language.

At once the angry lines about the corners of his mouth softened and seemed to melt away. It transformed his unattractive face.

The girl took up my tray and silently withdrew. O'Malloran waited until she had returned to the kitchen outside; then he raised one of his large, scarred hands and pointed to the doorway through which she had passed.

'Then you are willing to let Brucknor spoil her life?' he asked. It was more a statement than a question, and it succeeded in its aim. I pushed back my chair and stood away from the table. The hurricane lantern rocked on its base. I groped furiously for the words I needed to distance myself finally from the man and his demands. I could not find them.

'All right,' I heard myself say, disgusted by my failed resolve, 'I will see the governor; but after that I am going home.'

CHAPTER XIII

The old flying fish boat was tied up against the jetty. A hurricane lantern suspended from the backstay cast a soft-edged circle of light over the stern of the vessel and the dark water just beyond it. The crew were asleep on deck. In the wider darkness at the top of the jetty, the village too was asleep.

The cacique roused the captain. 'The wind is good,' he said simply. There was a dinghy made fast to the larger vessel. The cacique climbed in and cast off the line. Clouds obscured the moon now, which had helped me find my way earlier in the night.

'I will mark the passage,' the cacique said.

He rested his own lantern on the floor of the dinghy and sculled out to the mouth of the little harbour. On the larger boat, the crew raised the jib and cast off. The on-shore breeze filled the sail.

I found a place in the bows.

'Put the case forcibly to him,' I heard O'Malloran instruct from the darkness behind us 'I am relying on you...'

The vessel passed a few feet from the cacique in the

dinghy. I saw him standing in the bottom of the little boat holding the lantern at arm's length, away from his body. The strong features of his dark face were lit up for a brief moment by the yellow light, the lines at the corners of his mouth etched deep with anxiety.

'Travel safe...' I heard him call.

One of the crewmen raised the mainsail and we drew swiftly away from Angelina. The captain handed me a tin mug of sweet cocoa. I sat with my back against the mast, the mug cradled in both hands, and watched the moon reappear at last from behind a wedge of cloud.

With the wind behind us, the vessel made good progress during the night and all the following morning. At midday, the first islands of the archipelago came up on the horizon. We put into the harbour at Grand Trinity just after three o'clock that afternoon. I washed as best I could and changed into the clothes I had collected from the bungalow before we left. A little unsteadily, I walked from the harbour to the small cluster of government offices which could be seen from the waterfront. The main street was almost deserted in the heat of the afternoon sun.

A wilting Union flag hung from a pole outside a clapboard building. I walked in through the open door and a young black receptionist inquired my business.

'I would like to see the governor,' I said. 'I have come from Angelina.'

I was shown into an adjacent office. In greater detail this time, I explained who I was and why I was there.

The assistant secretary pushed aside the file which lay in front of him and listened politely.

'It is usual for journalists to make an appointment before they arrive,' he said.

'It is not easy to send a message from Angelina,' I replied. 'And this is a matter of urgency.' I fished a dog-eared card out of my wallet.

The assistant secretary wished to be helpful. 'I will ask whether His Excellency can see you today,' he said.

I waited alone in the office. Time passed slowly. Through the open window behind the secretary's desk, I could see the harbour and, moored now beyond the customs house, the boat which had brought me from Angelina and now waited to take me back. It was hot in the office and I could feel the sweat gathering at the back of my neck. I was suddenly consumed with a wild fury at the fecklessness of my own behaviour. I had made it quite clear to O'Malloran from the beginning that I would not be drawn into any of his various purposes: yet here I was in a place I had no wish to be, bearing an unwanted burden on behalf of a people I scarcely knew.

I took out one of the handkerchiefs Justine had given me to mop my face. The fine white linen was stained now with tar from the deck planking of the boat. 'You can never decide on something and stick to it,' she had told me in the past, and I knew that she was right. If I left now, I thought, if I just walked out of the building and down to where the boat waited for me – and if the schooner from Manzanilla arrived within the next day or two – I could be back in London by the end of the week.

The door behind me opened and a young Englishman dressed in khaki shorts and a bush jacket walked into the room with my card in his hand.

'My name's Patterson,' he said. 'I'm the governor. I believe you want to see me. I've got twenty minutes.'

I introduced myself. 'Yes,' the governor said. 'I read your column whenever I can. Let's go into my office.'

It was not at all as I might have imagined it – neither the man nor his surroundings. In their twilight years, the unfashionable remnants of Empire had acquired an informal aspect. The stiff, aloof colonial administrators my parents had occasionally invited to Sans Souci were gone for ever. In their place were modern men with different goals and different ways of achieving them.

In the governor's office, we sat on chairs which faced away from the houses of the little capital town to a stretch of green mangroves and a grid network of shimmering salt ponds.

I said: 'I've been on Angelina for the past two weeks. An American company is about to build a hotel there. I believe it is a bad idea and should be stopped.'

It was evident immediately, though he might visit only once a year, that the young governor was well informed about the island for which he held responsibility. He knew all about O'Malloran as well. He smiled.

'I would guess a certain former priest is somewhere behind your visit,' he said briskly. 'We know him well. I have never doubted that his motives are selfless but he is on the wrong track – and so are you if you believe that thought has not been given to the future of the island. Her Majesty's government takes its remaining territorial responsibilities seriously.'

There was a jug of grapefruit juice on a tray on his desk. He filled two glasses, added ice from a bowl and passed one of the drinks to me.

'The fact is the whole trend of things in the Caribbean these days is geared towards opening up the smaller islands to the benefits of tourism. The opportunities are good. The only cards these places hold are their climate and their beaches – and they must make the best use of them or they will lose out to the next island down the stream. Since we can't get them to settle here on Grand Trinity, a well run, Miami-style hotel is precisely what the Angelinos need to bring in the tourists and their dollars.'

The grapefruit juice was cold and sweet. I put my empty glass back on the tray. The governor leant over and filled it again.

'That may be one view,' I said evenly, 'but I don't believe it's how the people themselves see it. I don't know about the inhabitants of the other islands down the stream, as you put it, but the Angelinos are not like other West Indians. They have a very different heritage. They are a unique people; they have very special qualities of their own. They don't want tourism. If you impose it on them, it will destroy everything that makes them what they are.'

The governor interrupted: 'That is a hefty assumption. What evidence do you have for it?'

'I have the evidence of what I have just seen on Manzanilla.' I said. 'I grew up there. I can compare then

136

with now. I had not been back for twenty years. I found a people changed out of all recognition: an envious, resentful discontented people. I believe, in a sense, hotels did that.'

The governor leant forward, put the tips of his fingers together and chose his words with care.

'Manzanilla's problems are transient ones. Tourism has brought money to the place and opportunity. In five years time things will settle down and it will all be quite different. The Angelinos may be an admirable people in some ways – but they are also obstinate. We have been trying for years to bring them into the modern world by moving the whole community to Grand Trinity. We would look after them properly here: they would have electricity and running water among other things. They won't hear of it.'

He struggled for a moment to contain his irritation. He looked closely at me. I was silent.

'Since the community insists on staying there,' he said, 'the willingness of an American company to invest in a hotel on the island is a godsend. It will vastly improve everyone's standard of living. The fact is we are not prepared to put money into the situation as it is at present. They have a choice: either they all come to Grand Trinity and we take care of them, or they make an economic go of their own island by opening it up to the world.'

I shook my head, but he smiled to show that he took no offence at my mistaken judgement.

'Look,' he said, 'you must understand that we cannot leave them as they are. I tell you off the record: the poverty of the island embarrasses us at the UN. Half the people don't own a pair of shoes. This hotel has FCO approval: it's a decision we have taken in their own interests since they will not leave, and they will thank us for it in due course.'

'There is no way to block it?' I asked.

'None at all. The land has been acquired quite properly by the hotel company from Katherine Lindop.'

'Katy Lindop?' I repeated foolishly. 'I thought it was Horst Brucknor who sold it to them.'

The governor was amused by my mistake.

'Not at all,' he said. 'I believe they approached Brucknor too, but he wouldn't sell. I'm sorry to say he takes your own view about developing the island, but for rather different reasons I suspect.'

He looked pointedly at his watch. I could see that whatever weight he might have given to my views at the beginning had been fatally undermined.

'As I said, Mr O'Malloran is well known to us here. I am sure he is a well-meaning man, but his judgement needs to be treated with caution. I think your own experience will have shown you that obsessive people are often people of limited vision: the wider issues tend to escape them.'

I leant forward to interrupt, but the governor had not finished.

'The Angelinos have turned down the opportunity to be re-settled here where life would be more comfortable for them. Now they've got another chance to progress. They can stay where they are and the money the hotel brings in will change their lives for them. There will be a substantial tax income, and we can build them a decent clinic and they can have a school as well. If we leave them as they are, they will simply slip further and further behind...'

'Behind what?' I heard myself protest; but the governor was looking at his watch again. He stood up.

'I hope you have a pleasant journey back to England,' he said amiably, holding out his hand. 'Perhaps next time you visit Angelina they will be able to accommodate you in comfort.'

It was meant as a joke, but I could not share it. I walked slowly down the steps of the building and into the heat of the afternoon. The streets were beginning to fill up with vendors' stalls. I looked out over the harbour and saw that a white cruise ship had dropped anchor at the mouth of the bay and was discharging its passengers. A group of local women in lycra shorts and high-heeled sandals had already taken up their stations on the waterfront to greet the first boatload of visitors. They took no notice of me, since it was clear that I was going in the wrong direction.

I boarded the flying fish boat as the first tourists stepped ashore fifty yards away. The crew greeted me quietly and left me alone with my thoughts.

It took us two and a half days to return to Angelina. The inconstant breeze blew at first from dead ahead and, with her flat bottom, the old vessel would not point into the wind. Every two hours or so, we were obliged to tack. Then, during the early part of our second night at sea, the wind faded and died altogether. Looking up at the stars from my place in the bows, I could see that we were making no progress at all against the weight of the Gulf Stream flowing north. At about three o'clock, the north east trades found us at last. I could hear the wind approaching; the sea rose and the captain took the helm himself. Angelina came up with the dawn on the eastern horizon. Later in the morning, borne on by the wind, we slipped easily through the passage in the reef, entered the harbour and tied up against the jetty. It was just after midday.

O'Malloran had been keeping a look-out for us all morning. He was waiting on the jetty with the cacique beside him.

'Well?' he demanded, even before I had stepped ashore.

I was tired. I had not shaved for several days and the stubble chafed the skin in the creases beneath my jaw. Salt spray flung up by the boat's plumb stem had dried and stiffened in my hair. My eyes were bloodshot and, to my shame, I had been sick during the course of the night after the wind had found us. As I walked up the jetty with O'Malloran at my side, the wooden boards pitched and rolled beneath my feet to the phantom rhythm of the open sea.

The cacique led us into his shop. His wife appeared from the kitchen with a jug of coffee and three enamel mugs. The coffee was sweet and strong.

'Well?' O'Malloran said for the second time.

'The governor will not stop the hotel,' I said wearily, 'He believes that tourism is the right thing for Angelina since the people have refused to settle on Grand Trinity. It will bring in money for a proper clinic and a better way life.'

I held out my mug for more of the sweet coffee.

'And there's something else,' I said, looking directly at O'Malloran's face. 'It wasn't Brucknor who sold them the land – it was Katy Lindop.'

And because I was tired, I heard myself add pointedly: 'I would have made a better impression over there if I'd been given the right information before I left.' O'Malloran had instructed me to put the case forcibly, and I felt I had done what I could with a bad hand. We had lost the game and now I wanted O'Malloran to acknowledge it.

'There's nothing more to be done about it,' I said. I looked across the table at him again. His face was chalk white now and I saw that his hands had begun to shake once more. This time, he did not trouble to conceal it.

He stood up from the table. 'You are wrong,' he shouted, pointing at me with a large, raw finger. 'There is everything to be done about it. We will stop them ourselves. And it doesn't matter a spit in hell who sold them the land: the result is just the same whoever did it.'

For a moment after that there was silence round the table. Then I heard the cacique say so softly that I believe he was speaking to himself: 'So Miss Katy was not one of us after all...' and he turned his face away from us to look out onto the dusty road and down towards the harbour mouth.

I knew that I had no strength left to argue with O'Malloran. I put my mug down on the table, hauled myself to my feet and left the shop. At the bottom of my hill, there was the sound of running feet in the road behind me. I turned and saw that it was Apparani. She had been sent to catch me up.

'The cacique want you to know,' she said, 'the schooner will call in the morning.'

I stood there in silence for a moment at the bottom of the hill, looking down at the girl's unhappy face. Behind her, through a screen of branches, I could see the finger of the jetty laid flat upon the green water of the harbour. Tomorrow, the schooner would tie up there to take on its cargo of smoked fish and copra. In the evening I would climb on board, the crew would cast off and hoist sail and by nightfall the little island would be no more than a shadow on the arc of the horizon. By the time I returned to London, my memory of the place and its people would already have begun to fade – the bright images displaced by the thought of seeing Justine again. Perhaps by now she had already grown weary of Luis and Madeira – perhaps she was already waiting for me in the flat. In the past, she had never returned from any of her absences to find me not there to greet her and forgive her. And I had always known she would not wait for long.

Then, like a man in a dream, I heard myself say: 'Apparani, tell the cacique... I will stay a little longer. I will not leave tomorrow.'

The girl shuffled her bare feet in the coral dust. 'I say thank you,' she said so softly that again I scarcely heard the words. 'Thank you, because we know you wish good for us...'

Then she was gone, back to her father's house in the village, her figure dark against the glare of the sun on the broken coral and then melting into the shadows of the galba trees which reached across the dusty road.

CHAPTER XIV

I woke at first light next morning, before Apparani had arrived. I looked out from the veranda of the bungalow and saw that the wind had died away during the course of the night. The schooner would be late. The little harbour was empty – but riding at anchor in the deep water beyond the entrance to O'Malloran's bay, there were now two white-hulled container ships. A thin plume of smoke from the squat funnel of the larger vessel rose vertically into the still morning air. At the stern of the ship, the surface water was stained with an iridescent film of oil. The rainbow colours of the oil shimmered in the diamond light. A chorus of disembodied voices carried over the water from the decks of the ships and, somewhere on the smaller vessel, an electric generator started up with a shrill whine of protest. From the galleys of both ships, twin streams of water, dark with the remains of the crews' breakfast and other matter, cascaded down the sides of the vessels and into the sea. In the channel between the ships and the shore, there was a purposeful movement of small craft ferrying equipment to the island. I could see that a bulldozer had already been landed on the sand.

I pulled on a shirt and a pair of trousers and walked down to the bay. O'Malloran was already there. I could see him arguing with a supervisor. The supervisor wore a yellow construction helmet with the name of his company stencilled on the brim. O'Malloran's metallic voice was raised in anger: the supervisor was trying to placate him with soft words. O'Malloran's face was pale and creased. He, too, had not troubled to wash, and his salt-encrusted hair stood up from his balding head in an unkempt grey nimbus.

Some distance away, in a wide half-circle like an audience at a play they could not yet fully understand, the people of Angelina were gathering in anxious silence. As I came closer, I saw that the men of the island had not put to sea that morning. I walked on to where O'Malloran and the supervisor faced each other at the top of the sand.

O'Malloran looked round at me and said: 'This man is in charge of the construction. I have told him we will not allow the machines to work... we will not accept them on the island.'

I could see that the supervisor's patience was beginning to fray. He had not been warned that there might be interference with the job he had been detailed to carry out. He turned away from the implacable O'Malloran and appealed directly to me.

'Look,' he said wearily, 'I don't know who you guys are, but I better tell you I don't make the decisions round here. My job is to clear this site and I plan to start this morning and have the area clean by tomorrow afternoon. I have a schedule to keep and I don't aim to fall behind on the first day.'

He pointed out to where the large container ship swung at anchor with the incoming tide.

'If you guys have some sort of problem with what we're doing, then you better speak to the boss. He's on that vessel and he can answer any questions you've got.'

Then another possibility occurred to him. 'If it's work you're after, speak to the project manager. He may be able to use you later in the week. I just want to get on with my job.'

I had woken up with a headache: the brilliant morning light pierced to the back of my skull. I put up a hand to shield my eyes from the sun and looked out again at the large white ship. The iridescent stain on the surface of the water had spread more widely; one edge of it was being carried inexorably towards the mouth of the bay by the incoming tide. The oil was dispersed too thinly this time to cause real harm, but I knew that it would leave its mark on the shoreline for a week or two all the same. For a week or two there would be little black pustules of tar on the sand beyond the limit of the tide and dark stains on the rocks at the mouth of the bay. It would stain the legs of the rock crabs and clog the gills of the anemones which lived between the tide lines. That was all, I thought – this time.

I heard myself say: 'I better go out and see him.'

'I will come with you,' O'Malloran added at once.

I shook my head. 'No,' I said. 'Let me deal with this alone.'

The cacique detailed two men to take me to the ship. I sat precariously in the stern of the canoe. A broad-beamed supply launch, on its way from the ship to the shore, passed close by on a parallel course. The canoe rocked heavily in the wake of the launch and I shifted my weight on the seat to steady the little vessel.

The platform at the bottom of the ship's gangway was unattended. I swung myself on to the wooden grating. The crewman at the top took me for a workman and let me pass. I asked for the boss and the man pointed along the deck towards the stern.

The vice-president had just eaten breakfast. He was finishing a cigarette and watching carefully the build up of material on the shore. He was a squat man with close-cut grey hair and a face burnt the colour of aged mahogany by a lifetime of tropical suns. He seemed pleased with the way the morning's operation was proceeding but, from long experience, he knew that it was unwise ever to show that he was pleased with anything. As I approached, he was in the process of despatching one of his aides with a message for the supervisor in charge of the unloading.

'Tell him to get off his butt and come to life,' I heard him say. 'I want everything ashore by midday and I don't give a damn if the schedule says one thirty. We can do better than that.'

The aide hurried past me and the vice-president was alone for a few minutes on the deck. He looked up at me without pleasure.

'Who are you?' he demanded.

I introduced myself, 'I am a journalist,' I said. 'I am

staying on the island. I would like to speak to you.'

'Look,' the man said at once, thinking no doubt that I sought an interview about some aspect of the construction plan, 'if you need information you can get it from our PR people. They're below somewhere; just ask. This is a busy morning for me ... I am going ashore in a few minutes.'

I could see the aide returning from the bridge. I came to the point.

'I don't need that kind of information,' I said. 'I just want to know whether you people are aware that everyone on this island rejects the idea of your hotel. They don't want it.'

The vice-president had built seven successful hotels for his company in various parts of the West Indies over the previous fourteen years. Three of them were on Manzanilla. As far as he knew, not a single person had ever suggested at the time of construction that any of his hotels was unwelcome. He flung his cigarette butt over the side and turned to have a closer look at me.

'What do you mean, don't want it?' he demanded. 'Most people in this part of the world are begging us to build on their islands. A big hotel on this little rock will put money in the pockets of the fishermen and their families. We will need labour to build the place. Afterwards, there will be all the hotel jobs – busboys, barmen, cleaners and so on. These people will earn more money in a month than they've seen in the whole of their lives. I've watched it all before.'

He smacked his hands together in a gesture of impatience.

'What's the matter with you?' he asked. 'Don't you want what's best for them?'

For a moment, I was tempted to explain. I think it was the belligerent set of his mouth that made me brush the thought aside. I knew it would not be something he could understand.

'The people don't want your hotel,' I said again.

The vice-president drew another cigarette from its packet, lit it and inhaled. I could see that he was trying hard to curb his temper. Without looking directly at me, he said slowly: 'Let's be quite clear about this thing: even if it's true that some of them haven't caught on yet, fact is there're less than four hundred people on this island, and they tell me that half of them can't read or write. What does their opinion count for in the scheme of things? After the hotel is built, tens of thousands of people from all over the world will come here to enjoy this place. Right now, I bet not more than ten of them have ever heard of Angelina. The hotel will put this place on the map. In two years time these fishermen will be screwing satellite dishes to their houses and lining up to thank us for coming here. They'll want the hotel then all right.'

I looked back towards the island. The slick of oil had been teased out by the tide into a narrow ribbon of iridescence which had already reached the mouth of O'Malloran's bay. The vice-president's aide rejoined his master. He ignored me. 'Boat's ready for you, Bob,' he said brightly.

The vice-president brushed him aside. He turned back to me. As if the thought had just occurred to him, he demanded: 'Just what is all this to do with you anyhow? I know about the crazy guy who used to be a priest. They told me he would get himself in the way – but no one said anything about you.'

'I told you just now,' I said. 'I'm a journalist. I'm here to write a piece about the island for my paper,' I lied.

'And which newspaper is that?'

I told him. At once there was a shift in his demeanour.

'Well if that is the case,' he said formally, 'I am glad to tell your readers how matters now stand here and you may quote me. This new hotel is another project of Eaglehall Hotels Inc. of New Jersey. We own land here on the island. We have had detailed talks with the British authorities. Our intention has their written approval. I can say this approval was given willingly and wholeheartedly. The British share our view that this hotel will serve the interests of all the parties concerned – and especially the fine people of the island themselves. We are proud to be here today to survey and then level the site. Construction will commence right after this is done. End of quote.'

I knew it was what I would have been given by his PR people in the ship's saloon, word for word.

The vice-president unbuttoned the breast pocket of his bush jacket and put away his cigarettes. 'Come back in a year's time,' he said without smiling, 'and we can offer you comfortable accommodation with a sea view.' But I had heard the same joke earlier in the week on Grand Trinity, and it had not made me laugh on that occasion either.

'I am going ashore now,' he said pointedly. 'I want to talk to their headman. It is not difficult to make people happy if you know what they want...'

I followed in the wake of the vice-presidential launch. The canoe pitched sharply and for a moment I thought that this time we were going to be swamped. In the launch, the vice-president looked straight ahead. I think he had already forgotten about his encounter with the uninstructed English journalist.

I came ashore from the canoe to find O'Malloran still arguing with the supervisor in the yellow helmet. The bulldozer had moved forward to the top of the sand. It was drawn up now to face the grove of coconut palms through which the coastal path threaded its way. It was the place where the foundations of the hotel would be sunk and where, as soon as the trees had been uprooted, work would begin.

As I approached, I could hear O'Malloran's raised voice: 'If you plan to clear those trees,' he was saying, 'you will have to pass over my body...'

There was a hoarse, almost hysterical note to his voice that I had not heard before.

The vice-president appeared at that moment from the direction of the village where he had landed. He was flanked by his aide and by the project manager who had come ashore earlier with the bulldozer. The supervisor turned to them gratefully for directions.

'This guy says the people don't want us to work here...' he began, gesturing towards O'Malloran. 'He says he's going to stand in front of the 'dozer...'

The vice-president cut him short. Without looking

directly at O'Malloran, he said briskly: 'Let's get on with it. I don't put up with trouble-makers. I heard about him. He will move soon enough.'

He said something else to the project manager, who gave a signal to the operator sitting nervously in the bulldozer. The man raised a gloved hand in acknowledgement. The big diesel motor burst into life. A column of smoke rose from the exhaust pipe above the cab and was caught up in the leaves of the coconut palms which formed a green roof over the place. The blade was lowered like the head of a charging bull and the machine moved ponderously forward. I saw O'Malloran brace his back against the trunk of the palm tree closest to the blade. He stood his ground.

The machine advanced until it was about thirty feet away from O'Malloran; then the operator brought it to a halt and raised the blade. He leant out of his cab. I could see the man's anxious expression beneath the visor of his helmet.

'You crazy?' I heard him yell above the sound of the idling engine. 'Get out the way.'

O'Malloran did not move. Everyone looked towards the vice-president.

'Tell him to get on with it,' I heard him say to the project manager. 'We've got a schedule to meet and I don't aim to let some unfrocked priest make monkeys of us. We're going to call his bluff.'

The project manager hesitated. He wiped the sweat nervously from the point of his chin. With a gesture of contempt, the vice-president shouldered him aside, strode over to the machine and delivered his instruction personally to the operator. The beat of the engine quickened again and the bulldozer began to drive forward once more. The operator lowered the blade for the second time.

Like everyone else there on the sand, I waited for O'Malloran to move. It had been a brave protest. but in the end it was bound to fail. The fact was that everything stood ranged against him: all the cards that mattered were held by the other side. Even the law was with the company: the land had been purchased legally and the British government blessed the plan. The hotel would be built because there was no effective way to prevent it. For the first time since my return from Grand Trinity, I felt sick with a sense of failure. I had been given a chance to block the plan and I had made poor use of it. For the first time I was suddenly aware of just what that failure would mean to the people of the little island and to their children. Not far away, standing at the head of his people, I saw the cacique. In the light of the morning sun, the man looked old and vulnerable.

The bulldozer closed the distance slowly to where O'Malloran stood with his back against the tree. His mouth was open and he was shouting something which no one could hear – but he did not move. From where I stood, I could feel the sand tremble a little under the weight of the machine. Then, suddenly, I knew what the man intended.

My recollection of what followed is like a length of film from which some frames have been unaccountably removed. The sequence of those images that remain are clear and fixed forever in my mind; but the whole effect is disjointed and scarcely coherent.

I will always recall, for instance, a high-pitched voice yelling above the racket of the diesel engine: 'Move. For God's sake move…' then recognising the voice as my own. I can remember racing blindly across the loose sand towards the tree, intending to grasp O'Malloran around the waist and hurl him out of the path of the machine. I can recall, too, shouting without hope to the wretched driver in his cab who could not hear me: 'He isn't going to move… he wants you to do it.'

But this time the bulldozer did not stop. As in the worst of all nightmares, my legs felt as if they were shackled as I ran so that I hardly seemed to move from where I stood. Fifteen feet short of the tree, I stumbled and fell, driving the point of my shoulder into the sand. Dazed by the fall, I looked up to see the broad steel blade approaching the tree and O'Malloran's body placed squarely in front of it. I saw O'Malloran's face twisted in fear, his arms raised on either side of his body: then the blade struck him just below the waist. The tree against which he had braced his back was levelled to the ground. The compact ball of shallow roots flung a thin curtain of sand into the air. Immediately, the engine of the bulldozer stalled and the raucous clatter of the straining engine was replaced at the top of the sand by a brief, unbearable moment of utter silence.

For some reason, my enduring memory is not of the fall of the tree and of the man in front of it: it is of the face of the operator as he leapt down from his seat in the cab. The skin over the man's cheekbones and at the corners of his mouth was drawn tight in horror, so that his whole face had become a staring, chalk-white mask. I saw him fall to his knees and vomit on the sand beside the tracks of his machine.

'He never moved,' I heard him moan. 'He could've stepped away, but he never moved...'

Then the vice-president's despairing, outraged cry echoed among the trees. 'For Christ's sake! The stubborn son of a bitch. He really meant to do it.'

That cry was followed by a very different sound. It rose, softly at first and then gathering strength, from the crescent ranks of the Angelinos gathered on the sand. It was a collective, unearthly wail of grief and loss. It swelled and intensified until it filled the grove of trees and echoed round the bay. The men out on the anchored ships heard it and, unaware of what had happened, paused in their work on deck to look curiously towards the entrance of the bay from where the noise was coming.

I knelt beside O'Malloran among the braided roots of the fallen palm tree. Blood from the broken body stained the sand around him. I took one of the man's large coral-scarred hands in my own hands and looked into his face. Blood ran from the corners of his mouth and, with each breath, a bloody froth spread from his lips. His blue eyes were wide open: I could see no trace of fear in them now. I felt his calloused fingers close around my own.

'You were not what I wanted...' I heard him say, 'but you were what came along and now you're all the people have. Are you... going to leave them when they need you most?'

Slowly, reluctantly, I shook my head. 'No,' I heard myself say at last. 'Not now.'

O'Malloran's grip tightened on my hand. I had seen him smile before only when he spoke to the islanders he loved. That mark of favour was reserved exclusively for them. Now – for one brief moment – he smiled up at me.

'I suppose I didn't really think you would,' he whispered. Then his grip upon my hand went slack.

CHAPTER XV

I reached out and closed O'Malloran's eyes. The party of Americans had gathered in silence on the other side of the body, the vice-president standing a little in front of the rest. Over to my left, I was suddenly aware of a movement in the loose crescent of Angelinos drawn up behind their cacique. The unnatural silence was broken again by that high-pitched, despairing, collective wail of pain. Then the ranks of the men and women seemed to split apart and people began to run towards the Americans. I looked up and saw that their faces were contorted by a terrible, unfamiliar rage. The man in the lead carried in his hands the short mallet that every fisherman took with him to sea each day. The dried fish scales on the head of the mallet glistened in the sunlight that filtered through the leaves of the coconut palms.

Still dazed by my fall, it took a moment for me to understand what was about to happen. Then I stepped over O'Malloran's body and stood in front of the Americans, my arms outstretched to shield them.

'No,' I remember yelling at the advancing men. 'No. This was not his way…'

The coconut branches which met in a ceiling above my head served to amplify my voice. The man with the mallet hesitated and then stopped short. He turned and signalled to the rest to do the same. I saw that it was one of the crew who had sailed with me to Grand Trinity – the man who had brought me water and a cloth to wash with after I was sea sick in the night. The grief-stricken face was scarcely recognisable as that of the quiet, kindly man I knew.

'It was not his way.' I said again. Then the cacique broke through the crowd and stood beside me. He said something to his people in their own language and, immediately, the man at the front let his mallet fall to the sand.

The cacique spoke again, more gently this time and, after a while, in little groups of two and three, the men and women of the island turned away from us obediently and went back to their homes. Soon, only myself, the cacique, his two sons and the four Americans were left there at the top of the beach.

'We shall take him up and lay him in the place we lay those we have come to love,' the cacique said simply. His sons fashioned a rough litter of fallen coconut boughs and prepared to carry O'Malloran away. The cacique beckoned me to come with them.

'I will follow you in a little while,' I said. 'First, I have matters to settle with these gentlemen.'

The burial party moved off in silence towards the village.

For a long moment after they had gone, no one spoke. Then the vice-president said: 'You may have helped us out back there. We owe you for that, and this company pays its debts.' He removed a new packet of cigarettes from the pocket of his bush jacket, stripped away the wrapping and flipped open the top. 'Every project I ever worked on had its own share of accidents – but this was the most unnecessary one I ever saw. I am sorry for it.' He lit the cigarette. 'We will keep our people on the ships until they have buried the priest; tomorrow we must get on with the work.'

I stared at him in disbelief. 'Get on with it?' I repeated inanely, struggling to control my voice. 'You think you could ever build a hotel here after this, with the hand of every Angelino set against you? Do you believe that a single guest would come to your hotel knowing what has happened – knowing that they would always be unwelcome on this island? Do you still have no idea of what he meant to them?'

The operator of the bulldozer and the other men were silent. They were looking out over the oil-stained water with shocked, unfocussed eyes to where the white ships swung at anchor on the tide.

'What happened was an accident,' the vice-president said. 'You saw it. In fact, if I was an unfeeling man I would say that the priest meant to die. I am sorry for it, but it was his choice and not the Company's fault – and, fact is, no one outside this island need ever learn a thing about it.'

I looked down at the bloodstained sand, conscious that I was being given a second chance. If I faltered now, O'Malloran's death would have served no purpose.

'If you go ahead with this hotel,' I heard myself say quietly, 'the whole world will know about it. People will read about the way you acquired the land, and how much value your Company places on the wishes of the men and women who own the island. I will see that the governor on Grand Trinity is obliged to hold an inquest: I will report it myself... I will write about it everywhere...'

For the first time, the vice-president's voice betrayed an edge of anxiety. 'I told you this Company always pays its debts,' he said. He leant over towards me and gripped my elbow. 'There will be no cause for you to write about an accident regretted by all concerned...'

I removed his hand from my arm, 'You still don't understand,' I said wearily. 'It isn't just a matter of what I would write. Before you build here you need the consent of the people – and that is beyond your reach. The land alone is not enough.'

The rest of the construction crew, who had been landing stores on the jetty in the harbour, arrived at that moment to join their project manager. They looked anxiously at the fallen tree and the silent bulldozer, unsure of what had taken place there but aware that something had gone wrong. The vice-president ignored their questions. He looked down again without expression at the sand where O'Malloran had died; then the reality of the situation was suddenly apparent to him.

I heard him say only: 'Get me back to the ship...'

I walked alone towards the village, following the path along which they had taken O'Malloran. In the little cemetery that lay between the foot of the mountain and the sea, the cacique was already choosing the site of O'Malloran's grave.

'We wish to lay him here,' he said to me.

'It is a good place,' I said. 'I think it is where he would have chosen for himself.'

'Now he will be with us for ever.' He looked down at O'Malloran's broken, blood-stained body. 'We think he gave himself for Angelina,' he said slowly, 'because he could see no other way.'

I knew it was what I thought myself.

They buried O'Malloran at sunset, which was the custom of the Kakwach. When the grave was closed, the people of the island approached to stand with their memories of him at the foot of the raw mound of soil.

The cacique said softly: 'It is our custom also for each father to bring a stone from his own piece of land to lay on the earth above the person they wish to honour. We will do the same for him, if you think it is right.'

'Yes,' I said. 'I think it is right.'

From the place where we stood by the grave, we could still see the two container ships beyond the mouth of the bay. The larger ship had recovered the bulldozer from the beach and had taken aboard all the equipment landed earlier on the jetty. Both ships were hoisting in their boats.

As I looked in the gathering dusk, their running lights came on. A mist was forming over the inshore water and the lights were veiled by the mist. I suddenly recalled how the lights of the evening traffic had been veiled in the same way as I looked out at them from my flat with Justine's letter in my hand. I knew the calendar would show the evening as scarcely six weeks ago – but it seemed at that moment to belong to the far distant, already half-forgotten past of someone I could hardly recognise as myself.

At the rail of the larger ship's open bridge, I could just make out an elegant figure in a chequered blouse and white linen slacks.

'Miss Katy is leaving us,' the cacique said quietly. 'She must have had one hurtful need for the money...' and he turned his face away from us again so that we should not see his own pain.

Yes, I thought – and so much for the special bond she claimed with Angelina and its people.

The ships hauled up their anchors. There was a flurry of broken water and, in succession, their bows swung towards the open sea. They came in line abreast of the cemetery and then passed swiftly behind the headland and out of our sight. I thought I had seen Katy Lindop raise her arm – in greeting or farewell – but it might have been a trick of the fading light.

'I wonder whether she will still get paid for it?' I heard myself say out loud, but there was no one now to give an answer.

'They have gone now,' the cacique said. 'You have sent those men away. In time they will come again. But we know they cannot succeed as long as you are here with us.'

During the course of the night the wind rose from the south west and the schooner, which had been becalmed all the previous day, was carried into the harbour and docked alongside at first light. The captain carried a letter for me.

Apparani brought the letter when she came in the morning to prepare my breakfast. The letter was contained in one of those elegant, pale green envelopes that Justine always used, and it had been twice readdressed. In the past, when she had gone away, the sight of a green envelope lying on the mat beneath the letter box of our flat would make my heart race with joy. I sat now on the veranda of the bungalow and used my pocket knife to open the envelope. In spite of myself, my hand trembled a little as always – for my joy at each letter's arrival had always been tempered by an icy fear of the news it might contain.

Out of habit, I read the letter first not carefully, word by word, but in a single swift scan of the whole broad sheet of paper.

'My own darling,' she had written. 'This is the first time I have come home to find you not here... your Ed told me where you had gone... for the first time I have had a chance to think. There will be no more Faro's, darling... no more Luis's. Come home now... the wanderlust is spent...'

Apparani brought my breakfast to the table. There was a paw-paw sliced in half with a segment of lime beside it, and a plate of smoked crevalle with boiled ackees and casava bread. When she returned with my coffee ten minutes later, however, she saw I had not touched any of it.

'You are not hungry?' she inquired. I shook my head.

'I will just have the coffee,' I said.

'You are not well?' she asked.

'I am well, Apparani,' I said. 'I will eat later.'

Satisfied, she smiled and removed the plates.

'I will keep it fresh for you,' she said.

I walked out of the house to the edge of the grassy plateau which capped the hill. Far beneath me, a little to the east, I could see O'Malloran's bay. The wavering submarine line that reached across the narrow mouth of the bay was broken in the middle, the keel of the barge that retrieved the bulldozer had carried away a section of the wall as it passed out of the bay. The limestone rocks which O'Malloran had so painfully built into place with his own hands, were scattered now across the pale sea floor.

I took a long, critical look at the thin line of the wall. Brucknor was right, I thought. The whole foundation is too narrow. The first big sea through the entrance will throw it over. I shall have to broaden the base. The cacique will find men to help me.

I recalled my first sight of O'Malloran struggling to lay his wall in his ragged swimming trunks and worn out shoes, the skin of his hands bone white and pleated like linen from too many hours in the water.

I can't manage the clinic like he did, I thought, but now I can get the governor to supply a nurse and a decent stock of medicines. And I can finish his wall...

In the afternoon, I sat down on the veranda of my bungalow and wrote a letter to my editor. I told him I would not be coming back, and then I added: 'However, I may send you a piece you will want to use about the British government's treatment of one of its smallest overseas dependencies. It is a bad story and I hope it will not be necessary for me to write it, but I shall want them to know it is an option I intend to keep open. 'Yes, I thought, I don't believe there will be difficulty about getting a nurse.

I sealed the letter and delivered it to the captain of the schooner for posting in Manzanilla. The schooner was making ready to sail, the decks piled high with sacks of copra. The sickly-sweet smell of the desiccated coconut jelly hung everywhere about the harbour.

'You not returnin' with us, then?' the captain inquired with surprise. 'I did not think you had a mind to stay – especially after they kill the priest...'

I shook my head. 'No,' I said. 'I am not returning.'

The captain was curious. 'An' what you plan to do here, then?'

'I will do what I can,' I said, as if speaking to myself.

'An' you will be content in this place?' the captain persisted incredulously.

The question took me by surprise. I considered it carefully for a moment, but by the time I had framed an answer the man had already turned his attention to securing his cargo and did not hear me.

I climbed the hill back to my bungalow at the summit. I halted for breath only once, at the final hairpin bend. Below me, the schooner had cleared the harbour entrance on its return journey to Manzanilla with its cargo of copra and smoked fish. The wind was directly behind the vessel this time, and I could hear the faint squeal of a pulley as the boom swung out over the water and the mainsail filled with the evening light.

The same wind that bore the schooner on her way riffled the leaves of the immortelle above my head and raised the coral dust on the surface of the roadway. I reached into my pocket and took out Justine's letter. I removed the letter from its envelope and smoothed the creases from it with the fingers of both hands. Without reading it again, I tore it in half and then in half once more. I opened my fingers and the fragments of paper were swept from the palm of my hand. They floated together for a moment like a brood of green butterflies reluctant to go their separate ways. Then they were dispersed by the wind and I lost sight of them against the green expanse of the rainforest and the sea beyond it.